Hannah and the Snowy Hideaway

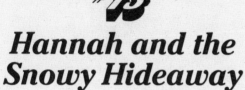

Hannah and the Snowy Hideaway

Hilda Stahl

CROSSWAY BOOKS • WHEATON, ILLINOIS
A DIVISION OF GOOD NEWS PUBLISHERS

Hannah and the Snowy Hideaway.

Copyright © 1993 by Word Spinners, Inc.

Published by Crossway Books
      a division of
      Good News Publishers
      1300 Crescent Street
      Wheaton, Illinois 60187.

Cover illustration: Paul Casale

Art Direction/Design: Mark Schramm

First printing, 1993

Printed in the United States of America

ISBN0-89107-748-0

01		00		99		98									
15	14	13	12	11	10	9	8	7	6	5	4	3	2		

Contents

Snow Days

With a long, ragged sigh Hannah Shigwam pushed back her long, straight, dark hair and stared out the living room window at the snow piled high along the curb. The big rock that sat in their yard near the sidewalk looked like a giant snowman who'd lost his head. It was hard to imagine that just a few months ago the yards up and down the street were covered with lush green grass and with flower beds of every color imaginable. Last week it had been fun to have a snow day and miss school, but today it wasn't fun at all!

Upstairs Burke was crying because he was teething. And Mom was trying to take a nap. The twins ran into the living room and caught Hannah's hands. They were identical twins with the same straight black hair, black eyes, high cheekbones, and broad foreheads of the Ottawa Indian. They both wore blue jeans and red sweaters with tiny white flowers embroidered around the neckline and cuffs. "We want to bake cookies," Vivian said, bouncing up and down.

"Chocolate-chip cookies," Sherry said, bouncing up and down too. She always did just what Vivian did.

Their enthusiasm made Hannah's head hurt. "So, go bake cookies!"

They gasped and looked around Hannah at each other, then back up at Hannah. "Without you?"

"Yes!" Hannah tugged free. "Now, go!"

They giggled with their heads together and ran back into the kitchen.

In the family room Lena was watching a video on TV and had it so loud everybody in the house could hear it. Lena was trying to prove she could do what she wanted no matter what Hannah said to her. Hannah had decided to let Mom deal with Lena later.

Hannah ran to the phone in the hall outside the laundry room, stepped inside the laundry room with phone in hand, and closed the door almost tight. The room smelled of soap and bleach along with the rank odor of Dad's dirty socks he'd tossed in the basket last night.

Hannah punched Chelsea McCrea's number, which she knew by heart. Chelsea lived right across the street. Chelsea McCrea, Roxie Shoulders, Kathy Aber, and Hannah were best friends and met together every day to talk about all kinds of things, share a Bible verse, and pray. When they couldn't meet, they talked on the phone. Chelsea was the only one with a phone in her room. Kathy was the only one who lived a block outside the subdivision called The Ravines.

When Chelsea answered, Hannah cried, "Save me!"

Chelsea giggled. "You save *me*!"

"Can you come over?"

"I wish I could, but I can't. I'm watching Mike."

In the background Mike called, "Come on, Chel! Mom said you have to play with me."

"I gotta go, Hannah."

Hannah sighed heavily. "Maybe tomorrow."

"Maybe. Unless more snow keeps us shut in."

Hannah slowly hung up. She couldn't bear the thought! Giggles drifted out from the kitchen. The video blasted out from the family room. Hannah scooped up the phone, ducked back into the laundry room, and jabbed Roxie's number. Her little sister Faye answered. "Roxie please," Hannah said.

"She can't talk long, Hannah. She's baby-sitting me."

Hannah sighed heavily. "Never mind then. I thought she could come over." Hannah's dark eyes lit up. "Hey, why don't you and Roxie both come over? The twins are baking cookies."

"Mom says I can't go out. I'm being punished for kicking a boy at preschool."

Hannah frowned even as she bit back a chuckle. "Why'd you kick him?"

"He said I didn't know how to read since I'm only four, and I said I did."

"I've heard you read."

"I know. I can read all right. Randy thinks nobody can read because he can't."

In the background Hannah heard Roxie say, "Who are you talking to, Faye? Mom says we can't tie up the phone."

Hannah twisted the phone cord around her finger. "Tell her it's me."

"It's Hannah. I already told her you can't talk to her."

"Give me that phone!"

Hannah waited, and an instant later Roxie said, "Hi."

"I thought you could come over, but Faye says you can't."

"She's right. And we can't have anybody come here. Sorry. Maybe tomorrow."

Hannah sighed. "I guess." She said good-bye, hung up, and slowly walked back to the front window in the living room. She gazed longingly at Chelsea's house across the street. She couldn't go to Chelsea's because she was watching her little brother Mike. Next door to Chelsea, Roxie was watching her little sister Faye. Hannah wrinkled her nose. The worst part of the snow was that it sometimes kept the Best Friends from getting together. She wanted the sun to shine and melt the snow and ice, but it would take a long time to do that.

Just then something crashed in the kitchen, and Sherry cried, "Oh, no!"

Hannah pressed her hands to her cheeks. What had happened? She waited, wondering if it was bad enough to check on. Then she heard another sound that alarmed her, and Vivian cried, "Sherry, you made me drop the eggs!"

Trembling, Hannah ran into the kitchen. The twins stood near the counter looking in consternation down at the floor. The flour canister lay on its side on the floor with flour dusting the counter, the floor, Sherry, and the step stool. Next to the flour a carton of eggs lay upside-down, yolks and whites flowing out across the floor. "Girls!"

They jumped, and Sherry dropped the sugar canister just as the microwave buzzed. Vivian opened it and yelped. Hannah could see that the whole inside of the microwave was spattered with margarine. There wasn't much left in the bowl. Hannah's heart sank right down to her sneakers.

Mom hurried in, still looking tired, and gasped. "Hannah, what happened?"

Hannah's eyes widened, and she pointed to herself. "Me? I didn't do anything!"

"She said we could bake cookies," the twins said together as they pointed accusingly at Hannah.

She glared at the twins. "How was I to know you'd make such a mess?"

Mom shook her finger at Hannah. "You know they can't work alone in the kitchen. They're eight, not twelve like you." Mom tossed the roll of white, highly absorbent paper towels to Hannah. "Clean it up."

Hannah's temper shot high, but she wouldn't let it get away from her. She wanted to obey Mom without having a fit because she knew that's what Jesus wanted.

Mom touched Hannah's arm and said softly, "You were in charge of the girls."

"I know." Hannah's anger oozed away. "I'm sorry."

"I know." Mom kissed Hannah, then turned to the girls. "You help Hannah. Do what she says." Mom shook her finger at the twins. "And never try to bake cookies alone again until you're a little older."

The twins hung their heads. "We won't." Vivian peeked at Hannah mischievously. Sherry brushed tears away.

Just then the phone rang. Hannah rushed across the kitchen to answer it, but Mom reached it first. Hannah wondered if Mom was tired of being snowed in too.

Sighing, Hannah picked up the canisters and set them on the counter beside the sink. "Get the dustpan, Vivian."

"I will," Sherry said. She ran to the broom closet and brought back the plastic red dustpan. She scooped up flour, sugar, and broken eggs.

Hannah grabbed the dustpan before Sherry could spill it down the front of the counter as she tried to pour it into the garbage disposal in the sink.

Mom turned from the phone. "Hannah, Ciddy Griggs wants to know if you can baby-sit her kids the rest of the day."

"Baby-sit? But Alyson is the same age as me!"

"I know, but Ciddy says Alyson can't handle Luann and Brittany." Mom covered the mouthpiece and lowered her voice. "Great-grandma Griggs is there and makes it hard on all of them."

Hannah wondered if she wanted to go there

or stay home. They lived right next door, and Alyson was in her class at school, but Alyson didn't have anything to do with her—probably because she was Ottawa.

"They really need you," Mom said.

"OK, I'll do it." Hannah dumped the stuff in the dustpan in the sink as Mom told Ciddy Griggs Hannah would be right over.

"Take us with you, Hannah!" the twins said together. They were tired of being snowed in too.

"You can't go," Mom said.

Hannah breathed a sigh of relief.

A few minutes later Hannah stepped outdoors into the freezing cold wind. She huddled down in her warm jacket as she walked carefully along the snowy, icy sidewalk to the house beside hers. This had to be a lot better than staying home with her three sisters and baby brother.

Then Hannah remembered how eighty-year-old Agatha Griggs with her sharp tongue and sad face had yelled at her the last time she'd seen her.

Maybe being at the Griggs family's house wasn't going to be better after all.

2

Terrible News

As she handed her jacket to Ciddy Griggs to hang in the hall closet, Hannah heard voices and glanced toward the family room. All the houses at The Ravines looked pretty much alike inside and out, though they were painted different colors.

Ciddy Griggs slipped her long, dark blue wool coat on, sending out a whiff of perfume. She usually had a smile on her face, but today she wasn't smiling. Her makeup was perfect, but it didn't cover the circles under her eyes. "I have to get away for a while, no matter how slippery the roads are." She flipped back her blonde hair. The whole family had blonde hair and blue eyes. Ciddy looked down the hall toward the guest room and whispered, "Grandma Agatha is in the guest room taking a nap—or is supposed to be anyway. When she wakes up, see that she gets a snack. She didn't eat much lunch."

Hannah looked toward the guest room. Her family used their guest room room as a study. She glanced up the wide stairs. "What about the girls?"

Ciddy shrugged. "I really called you over to keep an eye on Grandma Agatha. I was embarrassed to tell your mother."

"Where are the girls?"

"Luann and Brittany are watching TV in the family room, and Alyson is on the phone talking to one of her friends." Ciddy opened the door, letting in a rush of cold air. "Grandma Agatha will be up soon, so fix her a bowl of tomato soup."

Hannah mumbled a weak good-bye as Ciddy Griggs hurried to the yellow car she'd backed out of the garage earlier. Exhaust swirled out of the tailpipe and seemed to hang in the air as if it had frozen in place.

Slowly Hannah closed the door and walked toward the kitchen to wait for Grandma Agatha. Alyson's voice floated out to Hannah, and she hesitated just outside the door. She didn't want to intrude on a private phone conversation, but what could she do?

"I know Eli likes me," Alyson was saying. "I'm sure he's going to ask me to go with him to his church's sledding party."

Trembling, Hannah clamped her hand over her

mouth. Was Alyson talking about Eli Shoulders? Hannah tried to walk away from the kitchen door, but her legs felt too weak. She frowned. There could easily be another Eli. Alyson couldn't mean Roxie's brother.

Alyson said impatiently, "Of course I mean Eli Shoulders! You know that, Peggy. He's the boy I've loved for a month now. He took me for a ride Friday after school." She giggled. "You know he has his driver's license now."

Hannah sank weakly against the wall outside the kitchen. Her head almost bumped a family portrait hanging on the hallway wall. She glanced at the smiling blondes—three girls and their parents, Reece and Ciddy Griggs. The picture looked totally different from the portrait hanging in the Shigwam family room—Chief and Beryl with four girls and a baby boy. Eli, like the other white boys, would naturally like Alyson better, Hannah thought to herself.

Hannah swallowed hard. She'd thought Eli liked *her*. For the last several weeks he'd talked to her often. He'd even stopped in her yard yesterday to talk to her when she was building a snowman. He'd been dressed in a bright red jacket with bright blue pockets and hood and gloves. The sun had been so brilliant on the snow, he was wearing his prescription sunglasses instead of his regular glasses.

"Want me to lift the head up on the snowman?" he'd asked. He was at least six inches taller than Hannah.

"Sure." She'd built the snowman so tall she couldn't put the head on without struggling. That always happened! She'd roll the bottom much bigger than she'd planned, then roll the middle ball to fit right on the bottom. By then the snowman was close to six feet tall!

Eli easily picked up the big ball she'd rolled and set it in place, then packed snow between the head and the shoulders until the head sat in place evenly. "I like building snowmen, don't you?"

"Yes." She pushed some black rocks in for eyes, then a carrot for a nose.

Eli used a curved twig for a mouth and short-needle pine twigs for eyebrows. He smiled at the face, then turned to Hannah again. "I like sledding too."

Her eyes lit up. "Me too."

"Want to go to the church sledding party with me?"

Her heart had leaped, then zoomed to her feet. She wasn't allowed to go with boys yet. But she didn't have the courage to tell Eli that. He'd think she was such a baby! "I want to go with you, but I have to ask my parents first."

"Okay." He smiled. "Call me when you know."

"I will." With tears in her eyes, she'd watched him walk back home. She knew she couldn't go to the party with him. But maybe she could meet him there—that would be like going with him. Even as she thought of the lies she'd have to tell to make that plan work, she pushed the plan aside. She'd tell Mom and Dad everything. They'd let her go, but she wouldn't be able to pretend she was on a date with Eli. And she'd have to let him know that.

She thought about that now as she listened to Alyson talking to her friend Peggy. Hannah nervously rubbed her hands up and down her sweater. She'd planned to call Eli this morning to tell him she couldn't date yet, but she knew he'd spent the night with a friend and was snowed in there. She just couldn't call him there. How she wanted to go with Eli no matter what Mom and Dad said! But she wouldn't. But she sure didn't want him to go with Alyson either!

Just then Hannah heard Grandma Agatha's cane thumping the floor as she walked down the hall. Hannah stiffened and slowly turned toward Grandma Agatha. Her green sweater hung down on her short, slight body and over her black pants. Her curly, thin, gray hair was combed neatly back from her wrinkled face. She leaned heavily on her cane as she walked. She studied Hannah intently through shell-rimmed glasses.

"You're that Ottawa Indian girl from next door," Grandma Agatha said with a frown.

Hannah nodded. She hoped Grandma Agatha didn't remember the last time they'd met. "I'm Hannah Shigwam. I came to keep you company."

"What's wrong with the family?"

Hannah didn't want to hurt Grandma Agatha's feelings. "Ciddy went away for a while."

Blinking her watery blue eyes, Grandma Agatha leaned heavier on her cane. "And my great-granddaughters are tired of me."

Hannah chewed her bottom lip, then finally said, "I'd like to fix you something to eat."

"I don't want to eat ever again. Why stay alive? Nobody wants me." Grandma Agatha's voice broke. "I'm old and in the way. Life isn't worth living."

Hannah peered closely at Grandma Agatha. Did she mean it, or was she only feeling sorry for herself? Hannah could remember when her grandma said things like that in order to make the family feel sorry for her. But Grandma Agatha seemed to be serious! Hannah held her hand out to Grandma Agatha. "Come have a cup of tea and a bowl of soup, and then you'll feel better."

Agatha squared her shoulders and lifted her head. "Why do you care, Hannah Shigwam?"

"I just do. So does your family. You're their great-grandmother. The family should love and respect you."

Agatha looked closely at Hannah, then finally shrugged. "I suppose I *am* hungry."

Smiling, Hannah walked Grandma Agatha to the kitchen. It smelled like cinnamon potpourri.

Dressed in jeans and a flowered sweater, Alyson sat on the island counter with the phone at her ear. She turned and frowned, told Peggy she had to hang up now, then slammed down the receiver. "Can't I ever have any privacy?"

Grandma Agatha walked slowly to a chair at the oval kitchen table and sank down weakly.

Her stomach in knots, Hannah faced Alyson squarely. "I'm going to make your grandma something to eat. We didn't mean to interrupt your call."

Pushing back her blonde hair, Alyson scowled at Hannah. "Why are you here?"

Hannah hated being where she wasn't wanted, but she couldn't leave even though she wanted to run home and never see Alyson Griggs again. "Your mom asked me to come."

"Why?" Alyson impatiently waved her hand.

"Oh, never mind! I'll ask her." Alyson started for the door.

"She went away for a while," Hannah said quickly.

"What? . . . Why?"

Just then four-year-old Luann and five-year-old Brittany ran into the kitchen. They stopped short when they saw Hannah. With Luann pressing close against her, Brittany asked, "How come you're here?"

"Mom left," Alyson said sharply. "Hannah's here to baby-sit."

Hannah wanted to snap back, but she turned to the stove to boil water for tea. Her hand shook as she ran water in the teakettle, then set it back on the stove. Silently she prayed for the right thing to say.

Luann tugged on Hannah's sweater sleeve. "Tell us a story."

Hannah stared down at Luann in surprise. "Do you remember hearing me telling my little sisters a story?"

Luann nodded.

Alyson folded her arms and leaned against the doorframe. "Luann wanted me to tell her a story after she heard you, but I told I didn't have any stories to tell."

"Everybody has a story to tell," Hannah said

with a laugh. "They're piled inside your head just waiting to be told."

Grandma Agatha laughed, and the others turned in shock and stared at her. "That's what my grandpa used to say to me."

The girls looked at each other in surprise. Luann and Brittany ran over to Grandma Agatha. "Do you have stories piled inside your head?" Brittany asked excitedly.

Grandma Agatha scowled. "Did I say that?"

Luann and Brittany backed away.

To ease the situation, Hannah slipped an arm around each little girl and smiled down at them. "I know a story about a girl who built a snowman."

"And a boy stopped to help her," Alyson snapped. She spun around and ran from the kitchen.

Hannah bit back a gasp. Alyson had seen Eli helping her build the snowman!

"Tell us the story!" Brittany cried, clapping her hands. Luann copied her, filling the kitchen with shouts and clapping.

Grandma Agatha clamped her hands over her ears. "Stop the noise!"

The girls instantly stopped.

Grandma Agatha glared at them. "Nobody's going to tell anybody any stories!"

Brittany burst into tears and ran away crying,

with Luann tagging after her asking her what was wrong.

The teakettle whistled, and Hannah grabbed it off the fire. She fixed the mug of tea and carefully set it on the table. Why had Grandma Agatha been so mean? "Do you take sugar and milk in it?"

Grandma Agatha nodded, then thumped her cane against the floor. "I want to leave here now!"

Her heart hammering, Hannah set the sugar bowl and jug of milk on the table. "You're free to leave anytime you want, aren't you?" Hannah knew Grandma Agatha took turns staying with relatives. She'd come for a long weekend to visit Reece Griggs and his family.

"The snowstorm stopped me from leaving," Agatha said grimly. "I planned to fly out this morning, but the flight was canceled because of the weather. And Earl from Detroit called to say he can't have me come for another week because one of his kids is sick. I am stuck here!" She sagged down in her chair with her chin on her chest.

Hannah sat beside Grandma Agatha and took her soft, wrinkled hand. "A week goes fast."

"Not to me," Grandma Agatha whispered. "I don't have anything to do all day long!"

"You have your great-granddaughters."

24

"They don't want me around."

"Luann and Brittany would like you to tell them stories."

"I don't have any to tell."

"Sure, you do." Hannah patted Grandma Agatha's hand and let it go. "Drink your tea before it's cold, and I'll make you soup or a sandwich. What would you like?"

"I'm not hungry."

"If you were hungry, what would you like?"

Grandma Agatha sipped her tea, then set her mug back down. "I'd probably like a banana sliced on a bowl of cornflakes."

Hannah smiled. "I'll fix it for you." Hannah pulled out a white bowl, poured some cornflakes in it, sliced a banana, poured in milk and a little sugar, then carried it to Grandma Agatha.

"Thank you." Grandma Agatha took a bite and nodded, then ate it. She dabbed her mouth with a white paper napkin. "I *was* a little hungry."

"Could I get you another cup of tea?"

"No. I'm fine, thanks."

"Would you like to play a game or talk?"

Grandma Agatha frowned. "Why bother with me? I can go to my room and sit."

"You'd get bored, wouldn't you?"

"What does it matter?"

Just then Luann walked into the kitchen with

her finger in her mouth and stopped in the middle of the room.

Hannah smiled at her. "Did you want something?"

Luann nodded without taking her finger from her mouth.

Brittany stuck her head around the doorway. "She wants a story."

"Tell them a story," Agatha said firmly. "I would like to hear one too."

Hannah slowly stood as she tried to think of a story. Usually she had one on the tip of her tongue, but Alyson's remark had knocked it off. "Let's sit in the family room where we'll be more comfortable."

A few minutes later Hannah sat cross-legged on the floor facing the rocking chair Grandma Agatha sat in. Their eyes sparkling, Luann and Brittany sat on either side of the rocker with their hands in their laps.

Hannah took a deep breath and began . . .

3

Agatha's Story

So Leesa got to help build the snowman, and her brothers didn't push her away again." Hannah finished her story, took a deep breath, and smiled.

"Tell us another story!" Luann and Brittany said together as they hugged Hannah so hard they almost knocked her over.

"I have a story," Agatha said softly.

Hannah's heart leaped. She pulled the girls down beside her. "Tell it to us."

"Please, please, Grandma Agatha!"

Grandma Agatha folded her hands in her lap and looked off into space. "Snow was different when I was a girl. It was deeper and colder and stayed on the ground longer."

"How come, Grandma Agatha?" Brittany asked.

"There wasn't big equipment to clear the roads like there is today, so when there was a blizzard we'd be out of school sometimes two weeks at a time."

Hannah groaned. She'd hate having that many snow days in a row.

"I don't go to school," Luann said. "But I will when I turn five."

Grandma Agatha sighed. "When I was five I was small for my age."

With a sad look on her face Brittany slid closer to the rocking chair. "Like I am."

Grandma Agatha looked closely at Brittany. "Yes, yes—like you." Grandma Agatha looked over the top of Brittany's head into space as if she were seeing back when she was five. "My brothers were all bigger than me, and they teased me about it all the time. One winter day, after a big storm, they said they were going to make tunnels in the snow. They'd seen pictures of igloos in a geography book and wanted to make an igloo. So did I. But they said I was too little and too dumb."

Hearing a sound behind her, Hannah glanced back to see Alyson walking in. She sat on the couch and crossed her arms. Her flowered sweater made a bright spot against the dark green couch. Hannah turned back to listen to Grandma Agatha.

"I put on my snowsuit, boots, hat, and mittens and ran outdoors. The snow was deep, but it was so hard I could walk right across the top of it. I could almost touch the wire on the clothesline. I heard the boys shouting and laughing in the big field in back of our place. They had shovels and were digging a hole in the bank of snow in the valley between two hills. I wanted to dig with them, but they wouldn't let me. So I got a little shovel Momma used to take ashes from the stove. I sneaked around to the other side of the snowbank, and I started to dig. I got cold, but I kept digging. Finally I had a hole big enough I could curl up in. It was snug and warm in there. I was real tired, and before I knew it, I fell asleep curled up inside my little spot. Well, my brothers finally went inside to eat and get warm. Momma asked them where I was, but they didn't know. Momma got scared and sent the boys out looking for me. They didn't think to go around in back of the big snowbank in the valley, so they couldn't find me."

Grandma Agatha chuckled. "They always acted so big, but that day they were scared silly. Momma sent Burt to the police station. We didn't have a phone in those days. Nobody did except the real rich or businesses. Burt came riding back with the police. Because of the snowy roads they had to come in a sleigh pulled by a team of horses. They looked all over for me. Finally I woke up. By then I was real hungry. I crawled out of my cave and walked around the hill. There were folks everywhere! I was shy, so I sneaked into the house where nobody could see me. I took off my snowsuit and fixed myself a jelly sandwich and a glass of milk." Grandma Agatha leaned back and closed her eyes, then smiled.

Hannah waited, but Grandma Agatha didn't go on.

"Then what?" Alyson asked.

"What?" Brittany and Luann scrambled up to either side of Grandma Agatha.

She opened her eyes and looked at the girls. "Momma walked in and saw me sitting there eating as happy as you please. She hugged me and kissed me. Then she yelled at me and wanted to know where I'd been. So I told her, and then she turned me over her knee and spanked me for not telling her where I was going. After that she ran out and told the others. The police left, and the boys came in mad as all get out. I told them I dug a cave just like they were doing. Of course they didn't believe me, but I told them to go look. So they did. That gave them the idea to dig a tunnel all the way through." Grandma Agatha laughed softly. "Momma said I could work with them. They started to argue, then stopped. We ran out together and dug the tunnel. It took us three days, but we got it done. All the kids around wanted to crawl through it and feel how nice and warm it was inside—just like the book about igloos said."

Brittany jumped up. "I want to dig a cave and a tunnel in the snow!"

"Me too!" Luann clapped her hands. She ran to Grandma Agatha and caught her hand. "Come dig with us."

"Yes! Yes!" Brittany leaned beside Grandma Agatha's knees. "Come out and dig with us!"

"It's too slippery for me today." Smiling, Grandma Agatha pointed to Hannah. "She'll take you outside and let you dig. There's nothing like digging a cave in a snowbank."

Hannah started for the door, then stopped and smiled at Alyson who was looking sad and lonely. "Want to come dig with us?"

Alyson looked surprised, then nodded. "It's sure better than doing nothing."

Hannah glanced over her shoulder at Grandma Agatha. Hannah smiled, and so did Grandma Agatha.

Several minutes later Hannah led the girls to the car-high and car-wide snowbank at the curb. They each had a short shovel. Dressed in red ski pants and jackets, the little girls started digging immediately. Hannah glanced toward her house and wondered if the twins and Lena would like to come dig too.

Alyson frowned. "What's wrong? Would you rather be home right now?"

"I was thinking about my little sisters. I think they'd like to come dig with us."

"Ask them!" Luann and Brittany cried happily.

Alyson studied Hannah in surprise. "Why would you want to bother with your sisters?"

"I thought they'd have fun with us."

Alyson shrugged. "You're strange." She looked at her shovel, then started to dig beside her sisters.

"I'll be right back." Hannah ran to her house and slipped inside. Heat struck her, and she pulled off her knit cap as she called, "Mom . . ."

"I'm here . . . In the kitchen."

Hannah hurried to the kitchen and asked if the girls could come outdoors. "We're going to dig a tunnel in the snow."

"How nice of you to think of the girls!" Mom smiled and nodded. "I sent them downstairs to play. They were getting too noisy."

Hannah hurried to the basement door. The whole downstairs was a bedroom/playroom for the four of them. She called down and told the girls about digging in the snow. "If you want to come out with us, come ahead. I have to hurry back out."

"We're coming!" the three girls called as they raced upstairs.

Hannah hurried back outdoors, thankful for the cold air. She pulled on her cap and ran to the others. They already had a big hole. Their cheeks and noses were red, but they were bubbling with excitement—even Alyson.

Smiling, Hannah looked at the Griggs family's house. Grandma Agatha stood at the window. Hannah waved, and Grandma Agatha waved back.

Brittany looked over her shoulder at Hannah. "Are your sisters coming?"

"Yes. They'll be here as soon as they get ready." Hannah picked up her shovel and cut out a block of snow. It came out in a solid clump. "Hey, we could build a real igloo with the snow we take from the bank!"

"I'll start it." Alyson stuck her shovel in the snow and picked up a slab of snow. She walked to the middle of the yard. "Is this a good spot?"

Hannah nodded. It was strange but nice to play together with Alyson Griggs. "Let's make it big enough for all of us to fit in. And when we're done, we'll help your grandma come out here to sit inside."

A few minutes later Lena, Sherry, and Vivian

ran across their yard with shovels. Laughing and shouting rang through the air.

Hannah soon left the digging to the little girls, and she helped with the igloo. Just as they laid the first layer of blocks, Chelsea and her little brother Mike and her big brother Rob ran over to help. Chelsea and Rob helped with the igloo, while Mike worked with the girls. The bright coats in the white snow looked like a giant flower garden.

Hannah set a block of snow in place beside Chelsea's. "I thought you couldn't go anywhere, Chel."

She wrinkled her freckled nose and grinned. Her red hair flowed over the shoulders of her green jacket. "We saw you out here and couldn't stand not to help. So I called Dad, and he said we could come over. So, here we are."

Rob stepped back a little and studied the igloo thoughtfully. He'd turned off his computer to come work on the igloo. "This is great!"

Alyson smiled at him. "Maybe we should forget the tunnel and just build the igloo."

Hannah had been thinking the same thing. It felt strange to agree with anything Alyson said.

Just then Lena held up her hand and shouted, "Look what I found!"

Hannah rushed over to Lena even as the others huddled around her. Hannah couldn't see what Lena held. "What is it?"

"A ring." Lena pushed her way to Hannah. "See?" Lena held a ring between her thumb and forefinger. Her hand looked cold without her mitten.

Hannah pulled off her mitten and took the ring. It was a man's gold ring with a diamond in it. "I wonder if it's a real diamond. We'll show Dad."

Alyson grabbed the ring. "It's on *our* place, so we'll show *our* dad!"

Hannah started to argue, then stopped.

Just then Grandma Agatha opened the door and called, "What did you find?"

Alyson ran to Grandma Agatha with the others crowding after her.

Grandma Agatha took the ring and peered at it. "Very interesting. This looks like Reece's ring."

"Dad's ring?" Alyson asked in surprise as she looked at it again. "It does, doesn't it?"

"He never said a word about his ring being missing." Grandma Agatha frowned. "I wonder why he didn't mention it."

Hannah's eyes lit up. Was this a mystery to solve? She loved mysteries! Was this snow day going to be exciting after all?

4

Best Friends

With Chelsea and Roxie beside her, Hannah looked in hushed silence at the incredible igloo they'd started yesterday and finished today. It wasn't as rounded as the igloos she'd seen in pictures, but it was nice. The short tunnel to crawl through to get into the igloo kept the cold air from blowing inside. Alyson and her sisters along with Lena and the twins stood next to Mike as he knelt at the tunnel leading into the igloo and peeked in. Rob was inside with a bucket to take out the last of the snow that didn't belong there. They'd smoothed the interior walls until they were almost as smooth as the walls in their houses. Finally Rob pushed the bucket out ahead of him, then crawled out. His face was red, and he was smiling.

"All done," he said.

Hannah clapped her mittened hands and

cheered with the others. Now they could bring Grandma Agatha here so she could sit inside the igloo like she wanted to.

As everyone talked and laughed, Hannah remembered the ring Lena had discovered yesterday. Hannah glanced around for Alyson to ask her about it, but she was crawling into the igloo.

Roxie nudged Hannah. "What's wrong?"

"I forgot to ask Alyson about the ring Lena found yesterday."

Chelsea pushed close. "If you have another mystery, let me help you solve it, will you?"

Hannah giggled and nodded. "Too bad Kathy couldn't come over today." Hannah had talked to Kathy on the phone, but it was still too snowy for her to ride her bike over, and she didn't feel like walking.

Roxie nodded. "I was able to come because Lacy was home to watch Faye."

Hannah thought about Eli and flushed. He was home too, but he hadn't come to check on the igloo. Maybe he didn't want to see her since she'd called him this morning to explain she couldn't date yet. She'd told him she'd be glad to go sledding with him and sit with him when they ate at the party though. He'd sounded disappointed and had said he'd see her there. Hannah wanted to talk over her feelings with Chelsea and Roxie, but she couldn't with all the others around.

Just then Alyson crawled out of the igloo. "It's really nice in there."

Hannah stepped forward. "I forgot to ask what your dad said about the ring Lena found."

Alyson shrugged. "It wasn't his. He had his on."

Hannah frowned. "What's he going to do with it?"

"Nothing."

"Nothing?" Hannah couldn't understand that at all. "Is it a real diamond?"

Alyson shrugged again.

Before Hannah could ask another question, Grandma Agatha walked up to the igloo. She was dressed for the cold and wore a long, red scarf wrapped around her neck three times. Her cheeks were rosy, and her eyes sparkled with life. She lightly tapped the tunnel leading into the igloo with her cane. "I'm ready to look inside the igloo."

Everyone cheered and clapped. Rob dropped to his knees. "I'll go in first in case you need help." He crawled quickly inside, then shouted out, "Come ahead!"

Hannah held her breath as Grandma Agatha

got down on her hands and knees with Alyson's help.

"I feel young again," Grandma Agatha said with a laugh. She ducked her head and crawled inside the tunnel.

Alyson watched her. "She's inside. I'm going next."

Mike and the little girls went in after Alyson. Mike called back, "Chelsea, it's wall to wall people in here. Don't try to come in!"

Chelsea poked her head into the tunnel. "We'll wait out here." Laughing, she jumped up. "Now we can have a Best Friends meeting."

Roxie and Hannah giggled. Chelsea liked to call a meeting to order every chance she could.

"It's about the sledding party Saturday afternoon." Chelsea pulled off a mitten and pushed a strand of red hair back under her hat. "I might rent a video instead."

Hannah frowned. "Why? We all agreed to go to the party."

Roxie twisted her toe in the snow and looked very serious. "Is it too cold for your Oklahoma blood?"

Chelsea giggled. She'd moved from Oklahoma last spring and was having a hard time adjusting to Michigan's cold winter. "No. I just want to see a movie a girl at school was telling me about."

Hannah heard a slight change in Chelsea's voice. "What's the rating on it?"

Chelsea flushed until her freckles all ran together. "R."

"Chelsea!" Roxie cried in alarm.

Chelsea lifted her chin. "Don't you dare tell on me!"

Hannah caught Chelsea's hand. "We won't tell your folks on you. But you know that God already knows what you're planning to do."

Chelsea ducked her head. "I know."

"Don't let Satan talk you into doing something wrong," Roxie said softly. "We all know how bad that is for us. God is your strength. He'll help you resist those bad movies."

"I know." Chelsea kicked at a clump of snow. "It's just that I want to see movies I hear kids talking about at school."

Hannah said, "When you feel tempted to watch a movie you shouldn't see, call us or Kathy. We'll help you so you won't watch it. That's what friends are for." She smiled. Before Chelsea had moved in next door, Hannah had been without friends. She and Chelsea had become friends, and then Hannah had become friends with Kathy and finally with Roxie. Hannah never wanted to go back to the time when she didn't have friends. It was too lonely.

Roxie nudged Chelsea. "Has anyone called with work for *King's Kids*?"

"Sorry. There's no work." The *King's Kids* were a group of kids who did odd jobs for pay. Chelsea had started the business when she'd had to pay a phone bill she'd made by calling her best friend in Oklahoma again and again. "I think they're all waiting until spring when it's time to get yards raked and spring cleaning done." Chelsea sighed. "I miss working. I guess I miss the extra money the most."

"I get really bored when I don't have anything to do." Hannah glanced next door. Ciddy Griggs had started to pay her yesterday, but she'd refused to accept pay. Some jobs were favors and not for pay.

Just then the little girls and Mike crawled out of the igloo. They giggled and chattered about how much fun it was to sit inside the snow house.

Lena patted the igloo. "I hope it never warms up enough to melt!"

The others agreed.

Alyson crawled out, with Rob right behind her. Alyson turned to Hannah. "Grandma Agatha wants you to go inside and sit with her for a while."

Hannah dropped to all fours and crawled through the tunnel. She felt too closed in. Her heart beat faster, and she suddenly wanted out. When she made it into the igloo she felt better. There was plenty of space to sit down beside Grandma Agatha, who sat with her scarf, hat, and gloves in her lap. Rob had dragged in a piece of indoor/outdoor carpeting for the floor of the igloo, so it kept Grandma Agatha from getting wet.

"Hi." Hannah smiled as she pulled off her cap and gloves.

Grandma Agatha laughed softly. "This is a wonderful haven! I've not had an adventure like this in a long time. Thank you, Hannah."

"You're welcome. But I didn't do much."

"You did more than you'll ever know."

Hannah sat quietly beside Grandma Agatha. The voices outside were muted. She heard Alyson laugh, and again she thought about the ring Lena had found. "Alyson said the ring Lena found yesterday didn't belong to Mr. Griggs. What will he do with it?"

"He told Alyson to give it to Lena since she found it."

Hannah frowned. She'd make sure Alyson did that very thing. "We'll see if we can find the owner."

"We looked in the 'Lost and Found' in the newspaper last night, but didn't see a ring listed."

Grandma Agatha smoothed her scarf with her wrinkled hand. "I have another story to tell."

"Good! Maybe you better wait to tell all of us. The others will want to hear it."

Grandma Agatha sighed wistfully. "Do you really think so?"

"I know so!" Hannah touched Grandma Agatha's hand. It was cold. "Maybe we better go to the house and have a cup of hot cocoa or tea."

"Good idea." Grandma Agatha tugged on her hat, wrapped her scarf around her neck, and pulled on her mittens. "I'll go first."

"OK. Can I help you?"

"No. I'm fine." Grandma Agatha got down on all fours and crawled out of the igloo into the tunnel and on outside.

Hannah followed as close as she could. The noise from outdoors grew louder the closer she got to the opening. She stood up and almost bumped into Eli Shoulders. Shivers trickled up and down her spine, and she blushed. He looked sooo cute!

"Hi." Eli pushed his glasses up and stepped back.

Hannah glanced quickly around, then froze in place at the anger in Alyson's eyes. Hannah turned away quickly and once again almost bumped into Eli. "Sorry," she mumbled.

"I like the igloo."

Hannah managed to smile. "Go in if you want."

"I will." Eli dropped down and crawled inside.

Alyson brushed past Hannah, dropped to all fours, and crawled quickly after Eli.

Hannah knotted her fists. She wanted to crawl after Alyson, but instead she hurried to Grandma Agatha, took her arm, and helped her to the house and into the kitchen. Once again Hannah thought about the ring. "Does Alyson have the ring with her?"

Grandma Agatha frowned as she sank to a bench just inside the back door. "I believe she does."

"I'll ask her for it then. The girls and I want to see if we can find the owner."

"That's kind of you."

Hannah shrugged, then pulled Grandma Agatha's boots off. "Do you want tea or cocoa?"

"Tea. But make yourself cocoa if you want."

Hannah glanced out the window at the kids in the yard. She'd rather be with them, but she'd promised Ciddy Griggs she'd help with Grandma Agatha again today. Ciddy had been pleased at how well they'd all gotten along while she was gone yesterday.

A few minutes later Hannah sat at the kitchen table with Grandma Agatha as she drank her tea. Hannah sipped a glass of ice water while Grandma Agatha talked about the igloo and how much she'd liked sitting in it.

"I wouldn't like living in an igloo for real." Smiling and shaking her head, Hannah set her glass down. "I need water and electricity. I couldn't live without a TV or stereo or piano. Did I tell you I take piano lessons?"

"No. That's wonderful. Will you play for me?"

"Sure."

"There's a piano in the living room." Grandma Agatha pushed herself up and leaned heavily on her cane.

Hannah slowly walked with Grandma Agatha to the living room. A baby grand piano stood in one corner. She gasped and lovingly ran her hand over it. "Do you play?"

"No, but Alyson does. So does Reece. I've always wanted to play but never did take lessons."

Hannah thought about Alyson in the igloo with Eli. Her stomach knotted. She forced herself to sit at the piano and played from a book open on it. She hit a couple of wrong notes but played it well otherwise.

Just how soon could she get back outdoors

with the others? Would Eli ask Alyson to go with him to the sledding party?

"Is something wrong, Hannah?"

She sighed and stopped playing. "Do you think a twelve-year-old girl could go out with a boy?"

Grandma Agatha scowled. "No! Be a child as long as you can. You'll grow up quickly as it is. And if you live as long as I have, you'll be an adult a long, long time—an endless time!"

Hannah liked the idea of being an adult—to be able to do what she wanted when she wanted, but she didn't argue with Grandma Agatha.

"I remember my first date. I was sixteen and looked so pretty!"

"Where'd you go?"

"On a hayride with Arthur Meede. He was sixteen too. I thought I loved him, but I didn't. I fell in love with Reece Griggs, and we were married just after I turned eighteen."

"Reece Griggs?"

"My grandson was named after my husband." Grandma Agatha walked to the window and looked out. Finally she faced Hannah again. "If you want to leave now, go ahead. I'll be fine by myself."

"Are you sure?"

"Yes."

Hannah saw the lonely look in Grandma Agatha's eyes again. "I'd like to play another song for you, if that's all right."

Grandma Agatha smiled and sank to a glider rocker. "I'd like that."

Hannah turned the pages of the songbook until she found a song she could play. She really wanted to be outdoors with the others, but she couldn't leave Grandma Agatha until she was feeling better.

A picture of Eli and Alyson sitting together in the igloo flashed across Hannah's mind. Impatiently she pushed it aside. She had to think of Grandma Agatha first, not herself!

Tears slipped down Grandma Agatha's wrinkled cheeks. She brushed them away and smiled.

Smiling, Hannah played the piano for Grandma Agatha.

5

The Ring

Hannah said one more good-bye to Grandma Agatha and closed the door. Cold air almost took her breath away as she ran to the igloo where the little girls were playing.

Where was Alyson? Hannah glanced around, then groaned. Eli and Alyson were walking together down the snowy sidewalk. They weren't holding hands, but their shoulders were almost touching. Pain shot through Hannah, but she managed to hide it as Lena ran up to her.

"Alyson gave me the ring!" Lena held up her hand that was covered with a soggy mitten. "I have it in my mitten so I won't lose it."

"Could I look at it again?"

"Sure." Lena pulled off her mitten and handed the ring to Hannah.

She peered closely at it. "Did you show Roxie and Chelsea?"

"No. They left before Alyson gave it to me."

"I'm going to take it inside and look at it with the magnifying glass."

Lena started to grab the ring back, then smiled. "I'll come with you."

Hannah looked one last time at Alyson and Eli, then ran to the house. It was warm inside and smelled like hot cocoa. Mom was singing to Burke in the kitchen.

A few minutes later Hannah sat at the desk in the study and peered at the ring through the magnifying glass. Lena leaned heavily against her and tried to see too.

"Look!" Hannah touched the inscription inside the ring. "'To Reid/Love always/Bess.' It's rubbed some, so the ring must be old."

Just then the twins ran in with the newspaper. Sherry dropped it beside Hannah on the desk.

While the girls chattered about what might be in the paper, Hannah quickly opened it to the advertisements. She ran her finger down the "Lost and Found," then gasped and tapped her finger on the ad. "Look . . . here it is!"

The little girls pressed even closer. "Read it!"

"'Lost. A man's gold ring with a diamond. Reward.'" Hannah's eyes widened as the girls squealed excitedly. "We'll call the number right away. It's a Middle Lake number. We're to ask for Joyce Baylor."

Lena pushed the phone into Hannah's hand. "Call! Call now!"

Hannah's pulse raced as she punched the numbers. When a woman answered, Hannah said, "May I speak to Joyce please? I'm calling about the 'Lost and Found' ad in the paper."

"I'm Joyce."

"My sister found the ring. It says 'To Reid /Love always/Bess' inside it."

"That's it!" Joyce was crying. "It belongs to my grandpa. Where do you live? When can I get the ring?"

"Now, if you want." Hannah told Joyce where they lived.

Joyce gasped. "We live at The Ravines too— one street over from you! Grandpa must've lost the ring when he was out walking."

Hannah set a time with Joyce, then hung up. She told the girls what Joyce had said and how she'd sounded. "She was really excited."

Lena clasped her hands together and twirled around the room. "This is sooo exciting!"

"I get to tell Mom," Sherry said over her shoulder as she ran for the door.

"Me too!" Vivian raced after Sherry.

Lena hesitated, then followed the girls, calling, "I found the ring. I get to tell Mom!"

Laughing, Hannah called Chelsea and told her the news. "Joyce will be here in a few minutes to get the ring. Want to come over?"

"I can't."

Hannah frowned. Chelsea didn't sound like herself. "What's wrong?"

Chelsea sighed heavily. "Mom caught me watching a video I wasn't supposed to watch."

"Chelsea!"

"I know, I know . . . I didn't plan to watch it, even after I borrowed it from Janice Borders, but it was just lying in my drawer, and every time I looked at the box, I wanted to see it more."

"Why didn't you call me?"

"You were with Grandma Agatha."

"Why didn't you call Roxie or Kathy?"

"I wanted to watch the video too much!"

Hannah gripped the receiver tightly. "Remember what the Scripture says? 'Resist the Devil and he will flee from you.'"

"I know. I just couldn't resist!"

Hannah twisted the white phone cord around and around her finger. "You *can* resist, Chelsea. You know that!"

"I know it . . . But I can't seem to do it." Chelsea started crying. "I feel so bad!"

"I know you do." Hannah brushed tears from her eyes. She always cried when Chelsea did. "The other part of that same verse of Scripture says, 'Submit to God.' Put your wrong desire aside and do what God wants. You are of God, Chelsea, and can overcome problems because Jesus is greater in you than Satan is in the world."

"I know." Chelsea was crying harder. "Thank you for helping me, Hannah."

"You're welcome. I'll be praying for you."

"Thanks."

Hannah hung up, blew her nose, wiped away her tears, then called Roxie.

When Roxie answered, she said with a sob, "We have to pray for Chelsea. She watched a movie she wasn't supposed to watch."

Tears filled Hannah's eyes again. "I know."

"I talked to Kathy. She said she can come over after a while. We can meet with Chelsea and talk with her."

"And pray with her." Hannah leaned heavily on the desk. "I hate when bad things happen! But I know the Devil is a liar and that he is already defeated! Jesus defeated him and then gave us the power to resist him! We'll remind Chel of that!"

They talked a while longer, and then Hannah remembered the news about the ring. She told

Roxie about it. "It'll be sooo exciting to return the ring and see how happy the man is!"

"And get the reward."

Hannah froze. The reward! "I'd forgotten about that. I think I'll see what Mom has to say to Lena about the reward. It doesn't seem right to take money for accidentally finding something."

"Money is money, Hannah," Roxie said impatiently.

"I guess so." Hannah said good-bye and slowly hung up. Maybe she shouldn't say anything about the reward. "But it seems so wrong to take it," she whispered as she walked to the kitchen.

She leaned against the island counter and listened to Mom and the girls at the table. Mom was feeding Burke while she talked. Hannah decided not to say anything about the reward. Sometimes it was wiser to keep her mouth shut. Dad had told her that often, but she usually forgot his advice.

Fifteen minutes later the doorbell rang. With butterflies fluttering wildly in her stomach, Hannah hurried to answer it. A woman Mom's age and size stood there with a tall, heavy-set man about Grandma Agatha's age.

"Hannah Shigwam?" the woman asked hesitantly.

Hannah nodded. "Come in. You must be Joyce Baylor."

"Yes." They stepped inside and shut the door. "And this is my great-grandfather, Reid Meadows."

Reid Meadows smiled. "I hear you found my ring."

Lena proudly stepped forward. "I did . . . while we were building our igloo."

Smiling, Mom walked around Lena. "Come in, please. I'm Beryl Shigwam." She looked closely at Joyce as they walked into the living room. "I've seen you at the library, haven't I?"

Joyce nodded as she sat on the couch beside Reid Meadows. "I work there three days a week. Sure, I remember you and your family."

Hannah felt Lena's and the twins' excitement. She knew they wanted to get on with returning the ring, but they didn't say anything. They knew it wouldn't be polite.

Finally Mom turned to Lena. "Give the ring to Mr. Meadows."

Lena lifted her chin and practically strutted across to the couch. She held the ring out to Reid Meadows, and he took it with a trembling hand.

"It *is* my ring," he said hoarsely as he slipped it on the ring finger on his left hand. "My Bess gave it to me the day we were married. She died six years back." He stroked the ring, then pulled out a big white hanky and blew his nose. "Thank you! I'm glad to get it back."

Joyce opened her purse. "We have the reward."

Hannah's muscles tightened, but she didn't say anything.

Lena stepped right up to Joyce Baylor. "I've decided I don't want the reward. I'm glad I found the ring and could return it."

Hannah's eyes filled with tears. She was so proud of Lena, she wanted to hug her tight.

Joyce looked at Reid. "Grandpa?"

"Give her the reward anyway. She can give it away or spend it."

Joyce held the money out to Lena. "Please take it, Lena."

"It'll make me feel better." Reid smiled and nodded.

Lena looked at Mom, then back at Reid and Joyce. "I guess I can take it." She smiled. "Thank you!"

Hannah could see it made Reid Meadows pleased to give Lena the reward, and it made her feel better about it too.

"Tell me about the igloo next door," Reid Meadows said with a smile. "I once built an igloo. I'd crawl in that one if I weren't so big."

The twins and Lena took turns telling about

building the snow house. Lena ended by saying, "Grandma Agatha Griggs crawled right in and sat down in it! And she's a great-grandma. But she's small."

"Grandma Agatha Griggs." Reid suddenly looked very excited. "Was her husband Reece Griggs?"

"Yes," Hannah said. "And she had four big brothers, and they used to dig tunnels through the snow."

"I know her!" Reid pushed himself up. "I'd like to say hello to her."

"I'll walk you over there." A tingle ran down Hannah's spine. Grandma Agatha Griggs would be happy to see someone her age.

Joyce cleared her throat. "Grandpa, maybe you should call first."

"Nonsense!" Reid shook his head. "Let's go, Hannah."

Hannah led the way to the door, slipped on her jacket, and walked out with Reid Meadows. "Grandma Agatha was supposed to go to her grandson's place in Detroit, but the plane was delayed, and then somebody got sick in the Detroit family, so she has to stay here another week."

"Good! I'm glad I lost my ring if it meant finding little Aggie again."

Hannah shot a look at Reid Meadows. Little Aggie?

A minute later Hannah rang the Griggs family's doorbell. She smiled up at Reid. He suddenly seemed tense.

Alyson opened the door and frowned.

For a minute Hannah couldn't speak. She forced aside thoughts of Eli walking with Alyson and said, "This is Reid Meadows, a friend of Grandma Agatha. He'd like to see her. It was his ring Lena found."

Alyson looked Reid Meadows up and down and finally let them in. "Grandma Agatha is right in there. Go on in."

Hannah walked into the living room with Reid Meadows behind her. Grandma Agatha was leaning back in the glider rocker with her eyes closed. "Grandma Agatha," Hannah said softly, "there's someone here to see you."

Grandma Agatha lifted her head and raised her brows questioningly.

Reid stepped forward with his hand out. "Aggie! How are you?"

Slowly she stood, then gasped. "Reid Meadows!"

He nodded. "I've thought about you all these years."

Frowning, Grandma Agatha lifted her chin. "I haven't thought of you once! Not once!"

Hannah looked from one to the other. What was going on here?

Reid reached out to Grandma Agatha. "I came to talk about . . ."

"Don't bother!" Grandma Agatha looked at Hannah. "Take him back where you found him."

A look of pain crossed Reid's rugged face. "Aggie, my girl, don't send me away. We're too old for such nonsense."

"You might be, but I'm not." Grandma Agatha turned her back on them. "Take him away, Hannah!"

Reluctantly Hannah laid her hand on Reid's arm. "Let's go."

"No!" He pulled off his coat and sat on a chair near the rocker. "You can go, Hannah, but I'm staying."

Hannah swallowed hard, then slowly walked out of the room. Why didn't Grandma Agatha want to see Reid Meadows? Maybe this mystery wouldn't be much fun after all.

6

Best Friends Talk

Hannah hesitated in the hallway. Should she find Ciddy Griggs and tell her Reid Meadows was here to see Grandma Agatha?

Alyson walked from the kitchen and stopped when she saw Hannah. Her eyes flashed with anger. "What are you doing?"

"Nothing." Hannah's stomach knotted. She wanted to ask about Eli, but she forced back the words. "Where's your mom?"

Alyson stood with her hands on her hips. "Why?"

"Reid Meadows is in with your grandma. I was going to tell your mom."

Alyson opened the front door. "I'll tell her. You can leave."

Hannah hesitated, then walked out. Alyson slammed the door, and Hannah jumped. She frowned back at the door. Alyson was so mean! How could Eli even like her?

Hannah kicked a clump of snow and sent it flying along the snow-covered sidewalk. Maybe she should call Eli and tell him she'd go to the party with him no matter what. She frowned. She couldn't do that, so why even think about it?

Sighing, she ran past the igloo to her house. She told Joyce Baylor where her grandpa was, said good-bye, and hurried across the street to Chelsea's. Kathy got there just as Hannah did. Kathy's green cap almost covered her blonde curls. She parked her bike in the garage, grabbed Hannah's hand, and walked to the door.

"I feel like I haven't seen you in weeks!"

Glad to push aside thoughts of Alyson, Hannah laughed. "I know! What've you been doing these two snow days?"

Kathy made a face. "Helping Mom clean house!" Kathy's mom was a schoolteacher, so snow days meant time off work for her. "How about you?"

"I told you about helping with Alyson Griggs's great-grandma."

"Alyson!" Kathy rolled her eyes. "I know Alyson. She really wanted to be a cheerleader, but she wasn't good enough. Now she won't talk to any of the cheerleaders or any of us trying to be cheerleaders. That's how she is."

"She likes Eli." The words were out before Hannah knew they were coming. She gasped and darted a look around in case Eli had heard her since he lived right next door. No one was in sight, and she breathed easier. "We'd better get inside."

Kathy nodded. "I sure hope Eli doesn't like her back."

"I think he does."

"Oh. Are you sure?"

"Pretty sure."

Kathy didn't speak again until they were inside the house hanging their jackets in the closet. "Eli's smart enough to know Alyson's not as nice as you."

Hannah wrinkled her nose. "He might like her just because she can already go with boys and I can't."

"You're right." Kathy squeezed Hannah's hand sympathetically.

"I wish my folks would let me go with boys *now*. Why should I wait? Nobody else has to."

"I have to. So do Roxie and Chelsea."

Hannah sighed heavily. "It's just not fair!"

A few minutes later Hannah followed Kathy upstairs into Chelsea's bedroom. Roxie was already there and was sitting on the desk talking about a book to Chelsea, who was sprawled across the bed. They both wore jeans and sweaters.

Chelsea leaped up and flipped back her mass of red hair. Her eyes looked sad as she forced a smile. "At last! Best Friends together again!"

"You don't have to pretend to be happy with us," Hannah said softly. She almost always knew what Chelsea was feeling and thinking.

Chelsea sank to the edge of her bed. "I know. I feel sooo terrible! I can't believe I watched that video when I knew I wasn't supposed to!" Her voice ended in a wail.

The others clustered around her and hugged her and tried to soothe her. Finally she stopped crying and wiped her eyes with a tissue. "It's so hard to always do what's right!"

Kathy sighed heavily. "I know! I always think I'm going to be perfect, then something happens and I'm such a brat! Sometimes I'm so mean to Megan! And she's only four!"

Roxie grabbed a stuffed rabbit and dropped to the carpet. "I have been so mean to my mom! Can you believe it?"

Chelsea's eyebrows shot high in surprise. Roxie's mom was great. "Why are you mean to her?"

"Because she's always so busy with her art. I want her to be a mom, not an artist!"

"She's both." Hannah sat on the chair at the desk with her hands locked around her knees. "I think your mom is fantastic. My mom is only a mom. When someone asks me what my mom does, I have to tell them she doesn't do anything."

Frowning at Hannah, Chelsea pulled her knees to her chin. "Your mom is always busy! She does a lot of things."

The others agreed, and Hannah felt a little better.

Kathy twisted a blonde curl around her finger. "You should be glad your mom's not a teacher. Do you know how hard it is to be a teacher's daughter? I am always expected to be smart in everything! We all know I'm not." Kathy giggled, and the others joined in.

Hannah's giggle died in her throat. "My worst thing now is being jealous of Alyson Griggs." Hannah could barely go on. "She likes Eli, and I think he likes her."

"I think so too," Roxie whispered. "I didn't want to tell you."

"Jealousy can hurt you and others." Chelsea absently traced a flower on her bedspread. "I've done some really terrible things when I was jealous."

"I guess we all need help," Kathy said softly.

"I guess so." Hannah turned to Chelsea. "We

can't be together long, so we'd better talk about
. . . you know."

Chelsea flushed. "Please don't bring it up
again! Why shouldn't I be able to watch any
movie I want?"

"Because it pollutes your mind!" Hannah
cried. "We're supposed to fill our hearts and
minds with God's Word so we don't sin against
Him. If you fill yourself with the stuff in dirty
movies, that's what you'll become."

Chelsea sagged against the head of her bed. "I
know . . . You're right."

Kathy laced her fingers together and looked
intently at the Best Friends. "We were coming here
to talk and pray for Chelsea, but I think we need
to pray for each other. We all need help from God
and from each other."

"I know *I* do." Hannah nodded. She didn't
want to be jealous of Alyson, no matter how Eli
felt about her.

Hannah bowed her head with the others, and
they took turns praying for each other. They all
knew God answered prayer, and they all knew
that when they were tempted to sin, they had to
resist the temptation and do what's right.

When they finished several minutes later
Hannah said, "I think I found another mystery."

The Best Friends laughed. Hannah was always finding mysteries.

"I mean it!" Hannah told them about Reid Meadows and how strangely Grandma Agatha had acted toward him. "I wanted to stay to hear what they talked about, but of course I couldn't."

"Maybe Grandma Agatha will tell you tomorrow," Chelsea said.

Hannah thought about that the next day when she walked next door to see Grandma Agatha. Ciddy Griggs answered the door. She looked worried.

"I've been looking all over for Grandma Agatha. I don't know where she is. I was just ready to call you to see if she was at your house."

"She's not. I came to see her." Hannah's stomach tightened. Had something happened between Grandma Agatha and Reid that would make Grandma Agatha disappear?

"I called Reid Meadows to see if she walked to his granddaughter's house, but she isn't there." Ciddy nervously brushed back her blonde hair. "Would you walk to Joyce Baylor's house to see if Grandma Agatha is on her way there?"

"Sure." Hannah hurried away. As she walked past the igloo she wondered if Grandma Agatha had crawled inside to be alone in a peaceful place. Hannah hesitated and then crawled in. Grandma

Agatha was indeed sitting quietly on the green indoor/outdoor carpet. "Hi." Hannah smiled hesitantly. "Is it all right if I sit with you?"

Grandma Agatha fingered her hat and gloves that lay in her lap. "Yes. How'd you find me?"

"Ciddy said you were gone. I thought you might be in here."

"It's quiet here. And I figured nobody would think to look in the igloo." Grandma Agatha grinned.

"Is something wrong?"

"I had a lot of thinking to do."

"This is a nice place for that."

Grandma Agatha unbuttoned the top button of her coat. "I'm sure you're wondering about yesterday with Reid Meadows and me."

"Yes." Hannah was bursting with curiosity, but she didn't let it show.

Grandma Agatha sighed heavily. "When I was your age and he was fourteen I loved him with all my heart."

Hannah's eyes widened in surprise.

"I was sure he loved me. Then Bess moved to town, and he forgot all about me. That hurt me deeply." Grandma Agatha brushed a tear off her lashes. "It's strange, Hannah. I thought the pain of that loss was gone for good, but it all came back when I saw Reid. It was like it was happening all over again."

Hannah knew all about that kind of pain.

"He wanted to be friends again."

"That's nice."

Grandma Agatha shook her head. "I can't seem to forget the pain he caused me."

"But that was a long time ago."

"I know. Through the years I did finally force myself to forget Reid. Later I fell in love with Reece. I was sure his love had pushed out the pain Reid brought me." Grandma Agatha bit her lip. "Yesterday he apologized for hurting me."

"That was nice of him."

Grandma Agatha sadly shook her head. "I couldn't forgive him."

"But why?" Hannah asked in surprise.

"It's too late. I suffered such pain, and nothing can change that." Grandma Agatha sighed heavily. "To think Lena found Reid's ring that Bess gave him! I'm sorry that ring brought us back together again."

"Why?"

"It brought back the pain. It made me realize I can't forgive Reid."

Hannah hesitated, then said, "Jesus will help you forgive him."

Grandma Agatha jerked around to stare in

surprise at Hannah. "Jesus? Do you believe in Him?"

"Yes. Do you?"

Grandma Agatha nodded. "Sometimes I forget to trust Him and do what He wants." She brushed at her eyes again. "I am close to the time when I'll leave this earth to go to Heaven to live, so I do have that in mind. But I forget that Jesus will help me in my everyday life too."

"He helps me all the time, and I know He'll help you. He doesn't want you to hold a grudge against Reid Meadows or anyone else." Hannah remembered what Dad said often, so she said it now to Grandma Agatha. "Unforgiveness blocks your fellowship with God."

"I know." Grandma Agatha bowed her head. "I don't know how I forgot that. Maybe that's why I've been feeling unwanted and useless. I can't believe I felt so sorry for myself."

Hannah patted Grandma Agatha's wrinkled hand. "Jesus loves you and is ready to forgive you when you ask Him to."

Grandma Agatha took a deep, shuddering breath. "Jesus, I am sorry. Please forgive me, and help me do what's right."

Tears pricked Hannah's eyes as Grandma Agatha continued to pray. After a while they sat side by side in silence inside the igloo. Finally

Hannah said, "Ciddy is worried about you. She didn't know where you went."

"I suppose I'd better go tell her." Grandma Agatha pulled on her hat and gloves and crawled out of the igloo.

Hannah brushed tears from her eyes and followed. Her knees felt wet and cold. Outside the igloo she jumped up and helped Grandma Agatha to her feet.

"God bless you, Hannah," Grandma Agatha said softly.

Hannah smiled as she walked Grandma Agatha to the front door. "Are you going to call Mr. Meadows now?"

Grandma Agatha nodded. "You know, Hannah, maybe God helped Lena find Reid's ring just so I could get this whole thing settled inside me."

"Could be." Hannah liked the idea.

Just then the door opened, and Alyson stood there dressed to go outdoors. She scowled at Grandma Agatha and Hannah. "Grandma Agatha! Where have you been?"

"I'm fine, Alyson." Grandma Agatha smiled and patted Alyson's arm. "Tell your mom I'm back safe and sound."

Alyson sputtered and finally hurried toward the kitchen.

Grandma Agatha turned back to Hannah. "Can you come in for a while?"

"I guess so."

"I have a story for Luann and Brittany in case you want to listen."

Hannah hesitated as she thought about Alyson. She was not going to be jealous! Smiling, she gladly stepped into the warm house and pulled off her jacket. "I'd love to hear your story!"

7

Another Story

Hannah stopped short just inside the family room. Grandma Agatha sat in the rocker facing Luann, Brittany, Sherry, Vivian, and Lena, as well as Faye Shoulders and Mike McCrea.

Grandma Agatha smiled at Hannah. "The news spread that I was telling a story this morning."

"That's great!" Hannah sank to the couch and crossed her legs. She was going to enjoy the story along with the little kids.

Just then Alyson walked in. She stopped short when she saw Hannah sitting there.

"Your grandma's going to tell a story." Hannah smiled and patted the couch. "You can sit here with me if you want."

Alyson hesitated, smiled slightly, and sat down.

Hannah waited for a prick of jealousy, but none came. She smiled. God had answered her prayer! She settled back to listen to Grandma Agatha.

Smiling, Grandma Agatha leaned forward and looked at Mike and the girls sitting on the floor in front of her. "When I was a young girl we didn't have a refrigerator. Nobody did. They weren't invented yet. But we had an icebox. It was a wooden chest type of furniture that sat in the kitchen. Inside it were shelves with a special place to keep a big block of ice. The ice kept the food in the icebox cold."

Grandma Agatha looked off into space with a soft smile on her wrinkled face. "One of my favorite winter things to do was to go with my papa and brothers to the lake to cut blocks of ice to bring back to our icehouse to store and use as we needed it." She leaned toward the children. "The icehouse was out back of the house, near the shed where we kept the buggy and sled. It was built special to keep ice frozen even during the hot summer. I liked to get ice when it was hot outdoors. It was cold in there. I would've stayed inside, but Papa wouldn't let me."

Grandma Agatha chuckled, then became serious again. "That winter Papa and the boys got out the big sled and hitched the team of horses to it. I sat close to Papa so I wouldn't be bounced off the sled into a snowbank. When we reached the lake, my nose and fingers felt as cold as the ice covering the lake. The lake was frozen as deep down as I was tall. Papa drove the horses and sled right out onto the lake. Then he and the boys used a big saw to cut huge blocks of ice out of the lake. They lifted the blocks up with ice tongs and loaded them on the sled. A block was so big I couldn't lift it at all!

"Back at the icehouse Papa and the boys unloaded the blocks of ice and covered them with sawdust and straw to keep them from melting when the temperature warmed up. I ran around inside the cold icehouse, careful not to get in the way. I knew that after all the ice was unloaded we were going to have a special party with plenty of buttered popcorn and lemonade. I loved lemonade—and I still do! Well, Momma never would let us have lemonade in the winter because of the high cost of lemons. But today was different. Today we were celebrating the filling of the icehouse. I couldn't wait to drink lemonade and eat the popcorn."

Grandma Agatha gripped the arms of the rocker. "But something dreadful happened. I was standing behind the ice when the others left. They didn't know I was there, and they locked the door. I was locked in! I didn't realize it for a long time, until I suddenly thought it seemed too quiet in there. I ran down to the door. It was shut, and nobody was there! I shivered and started crying. I knew I couldn't get out once the door was locked. I knew that even if I pounded on the door and screamed at the top of my lungs nobody would hear me, but I pounded and screamed anyway. I pounded so hard, my hands hurt. I screamed so loud, my throat ached. Finally I gave up and huddled at the door, sobbing and shivering. I didn't know how long it would take Momma to realize I was missing. She'd never think to look in the icehouse. I had been forbidden to play there because it was too dangerous. She expected me to obey. I was wishing I had obeyed now! I told Jesus how sorry I was, and I asked Him to send help.

"In the house while everybody was drinking lemonade with fresh ice chilling it and eating hot buttered popcorn, Momma suddenly realized I was missing. 'Where's Aggie?' she asked my papa and my brothers. They said they didn't know. She got scared. 'Did she come back from the lake with you?' She was really scared now. She didn't want me to fall through one of the holes in the ice at the lake. A boy we knew had fallen right through a hole the winter before and had drowned! Momma was afraid that might have happened to me. I'd had to beg and beg before she'd let me go with Papa and the boys to the lake because she knew they'd be busy with the ice and forget to watch me. I'd promised I'd watch myself. Now she was sure they'd left me behind. But Papa assured her they hadn't. 'We'll find Aggie,' Papa said.

"Well, I was in the icehouse just crying my eyes out—more afraid of missing out on the lemonade than freezing to death. I knew how much my brothers liked lemonade. They wouldn't care if I didn't get my share. But *I* cared! We got lemonade only about three times a year because of the high price of lemons. Oh, but I wanted that lemonade!"

Grandma Agatha rocked for a while. She sighed heavily and continued, "Papa finally thought to look in the icehouse. When I heard the latch lift, I jumped up. Papa opened the door, and I leaped right into his arms and clung to his neck. 'Did anybody drink my lemonade?' I asked between sobs. 'Aggie, Aggie . . . I'm sure glad I found you,' Papa said with tears in his eyes. 'My lemonade, Papa! Did anybody drink it?' Papa chuckled and kissed my cold cheek. 'No, Aggie. I set a tall glass aside just for you.' I hugged Papa hard, then raced to the house for my icy cold lemonade! It was a grand day."

Grandma Agatha pushed herself up and leaned heavily on her cane. "I bought us some lemons so we could have lemonade and popcorn today. Shall we go into the kitchen?"

Feeling as if they were still back in time, Hannah and Alyson smiled at each other and followed Grandma Agatha and the kids to the kitchen. From the refrigerator Grandma Agatha lifted a bucket of lemonade with sliced lemons floating on top with the ice cubes. She filled glasses with lemonade, then pulled a large wooden bowl of already popped corn from the oven. The smell filled the kitchen.

As the others laughed and talked, Hannah sipped the lemonade and shivered at the sour taste. It was the best lemonade she'd ever had! She ate a handful of popcorn. What would it have felt like to live so many years ago?

Alyson leaned against the counter beside Hannah. "What would it feel like to live back then?"

Hannah laughed. "I was just thinking the same thing!" She set down her glass as she watched the little kids clustered around Grandma Agatha. She was smiling and talking—not at all sad and lonely like a couple of days ago. Hannah glanced around the kitchen and back to Alyson. "I don't think I'd like to live back then. No refrigerator. No dishwasher. And no malls to shop at!"

Hannah shook her head. "No, I wouldn't want to live back then."

"I guess you're right. It's just that Grandma Agatha's life sounds like so much fun. I wish my life was fun."

"It *is* fun! Tomorrow's the sledding party." Hannah wanted to grab back the words. Why had she brought that up?

Alyson got a funny look on her face. "How did you know I was going?"

"You told me."

Alyson flipped back her hair and laughed softly. "That's right, I did. I'm going with Eli Shoulders, you know. Isn't he just the cutest boy alive?"

Hannah barely nodded. "I have to go. Tell your grandma good-bye for me."

"Did I say something to upset you?" Alyson asked innocently. Then she laughed and turned her back.

Hannah rushed to get her jacket, then ran across the yard. She stopped at the igloo, hesitated a while, and crawled inside. She sat on the carpet and pulled her knees to her chest. Giant tears welled up in her eyes. Alyson was going to the party with Eli!

Just then Chelsea crawled into the igloo and sat beside Hannah. "I saw you crawl in here."

Hannah brushed at her tears. "Alyson Griggs is going to the party with Eli!"

"I'm sooo sorry."

"How can I even go?"

"Go with me!"

"Eli and Alyson will be together, and I'll see them. It'll hurt sooo much!"

Chelsea put her arm around Hannah and sat without saying a word.

Finally Hannah dried her tears. "I guess we better get out of here."

"I guess."

But they didn't move. Hannah whispered, "Sometimes I wish I had stayed little like the twins."

"Me too." Chelsea rubbed a finger over the stiff green carpet. "Then other times I'd like to skip over all these years and be twenty-two and out of college and on my own."

"Me too." Hannah nodded. "I try to look that far ahead, but I can't. The future is a fuzzy, dark place. My dad says as I get closer to it, I'll know where I'm going and what I'll be doing. Sometimes it's really scary and other times exciting."

"I wish it would just happen without any thought on my part."

"But that can't happen. We have to make the choices along the way that will get us where we're going." Hannah giggled. "That's what my dad always says to me."

"My dad says the same thing." Chelsea giggled. "Do all dads do that?"

"I'm glad mine does. It makes the future less scary."

"I know."

"I guess I can leave now."

"Me too. I'll go first." Chelsea looked around. "It's nice in here, but I wouldn't want to spend my life this way."

Hannah laughed as Chelsea crawled out. Hannah followed and stood up outside the igloo. She glanced toward Alyson's house and quickly away. "I'm not going tomorrow."

"What? You can't miss the party just because of Eli and Alyson!"

"Why?"

"The sledding party will be fun. Roxie and Kathy and I will be there with you. We can have fun together." Chelsea clasped her hands together and widened her eyes. "Please, Hannah. Don't stay home tomorrow! Please, please, please!"

Hannah laughed. Chelsea looked like a puppy begging for food. "How can I say no to that face? Sure, I'll go. You'll just have to help me have fun."

"I will! And so will Roxie and Kathy. You'll see!"

Hannah knew Best Friends would do just that—help her have fun. Best friends were like that. Laughing, Hannah ran to her house while Chelsea ran to hers.

8

The Sledding Party

With her round, red saucer-sled in her hand, Hannah stood at the top of the hill along with the Best Friends, behind a line of kids waiting for a turn to slide down the long snow-covered hill that sloped steeply on both sides. The hilltop was covered with laughing, shouting people of all ages holding or dragging sleds of all kinds and colors. One side of the hill was for toboggans and had several toboggan runs, the other side for sleds. The hill was at the edge of town near the golf course. People came from miles around just to slide on it.

"I'm cold!" Kathy's breath hung in the air, and the tip of her nose was red.

"Did you wear your insulated underwear?" Roxie asked.

"No! I would rather freeze!"

Chelsea giggled. "I have mine on. They're covered with tiny flowers and look real cute. This Oklahoma blood couldn't survive without extra protection."

Hannah laughed along with the others, then stopped mid-chuckle as she saw Eli and Alyson trudging up the end of the hill on the path that led to the top. Eli wore his red jacket with the blue pockets, and Alyson wore a bright yellow jacket. "They're here," she whispered hoarsely. Her knees buckled, and she almost sank to the snow. She'd thought she could handle it, but she couldn't. "I have to get out of here!"

"You can't." Chelsea gripped Hannah's arm. "You came on the church bus, and you have to leave on the church bus."

Kathy leaned against Hannah. "We're with you, remember?"

Hannah nodded and stiffened her knees.

"Hey, it's our turn to go next. Forget about those two. Let's have some fun!" Roxie dropped her sled at the top of the run. She sat cross-legged on the red saucer and clung to the sides. "Give me a shove, Kathy!"

"Get ready!" Kathy pushed Roxie on the back, and Roxie whizzed down the steep run. Toward the bottom the saucer whirled around and around, then reached the bottom and shot across the flat ground. Roxie didn't fall off like many of the others had.

"I'm ready." Giggling, Kathy sat on her blue plastic sled and held the rope.

"Enjoy the ride!" Chelsea pushed Kathy's back, and the sled zoomed down the slope. Her scream floated back up to Chelsea and Hannah.

Her eyes wide with excitement, Chelsea dropped to her sled and looked over her shoulder at Hannah. "This is sooo scary!"

"But fun." Hannah giggled and pushed Chelsea, sending her speeding down the hill. Chelsea screamed.

Hannah glanced over her shoulder. Eli and Alyson were looking right at her! She sat cross-legged on her round saucer, used her hands to push away, then sped down the long hill toward the flat land where the Best Friends were waiting for her. Were Eli and Alyson watching her and making fun of her? Was Alyson hoping she'd wipe out and land on her face in the snow?

Her cheeks burning, Hannah reached the bottom without enjoying the trip down and thankfully without falling off. She jumped off her saucer and picked it up for the long trek back up the hill.

The Best Friends surrounded Hannah. "You

can't let them ruin your fun," Chelsea said, shaking her finger at Hannah.

Hannah took a deep breath. "I know. And I won't! Let's walk right back up and go down again."

Just then they heard someone sobbing. They turned around to find a girl no older than six sitting in the snow and crying into her soggy, blue mittens. The Best Friends dropped down beside her.

"What's wrong?" Hannah asked softly.

"Can we help you?" the others asked together.

The girl lifted her head. Her eyes were big and brown with long dark lashes and perfect eyebrows. "I can't talk to strangers."

"We know. But we won't hurt you. Honest. We want to know why you're crying."

The girl puckered up to cry again.

"What's your name?" Chelsea asked in her Oklahoma accent.

The girl studied the Best Friends for a long time. All around them people were laughing and talking and heading back for the path that led up the side of the hill. "Donna. I'm Donna Workman."

"I'm Hannah, and that's Roxie, Chelsea, and Kathy. We're best friends. We want to help you if you need help."

Chelsea touched Donna's arm. "Do you need help?"

Donna slowly nodded. "I can't find my sister Susan. I came down on a sled with a girl I never saw before. I wasn't supposed to, but I did it anyway. I don't know where Susan went."

Hannah motioned toward the hill. "She's probably on top of the hill looking for you. What does she look like?"

"Like me, only she's bigger."

"Let's walk up the hill and look." Hannah took Donna's hand and walked with the others toward the path that led up the hill.

Donna looked up at Hannah. "If Susan's not on the hill, can I ride down with you?"

Hannah hesitated, glanced at the others, then back at Donna. Was it wise to take Donna back down if her sister was looking for her? But what did it matter? Maybe Susan was at the bottom of the hill. Hannah smiled and shrugged. "I guess so."

At the top of the hill Hannah and the Best Friends led Donna back and forth across the top of the hill looking for Susan. Hannah's stomach knotted each time she thought she saw Eli and Alyson in the crowd. But she never actually saw them. Maybe they'd already gone down the hill. Hannah relaxed and watched three toboggans loaded with kids speed down the toboggan runs. One tipped, spilling the riders into a snowdrift. They jumped up, laughing and brushing snow off.

Kathy giggled as she watched them set the toboggan back on the run. "That looks like fun."

"Not to me." Roxie shivered. "I hate falling in the snow."

Donna jumped up and down and shouted, "I want to ride a toboggan!"

"Do you see Susan?" Chelsea asked.

Donna stopped jumping and looked around. "Nope."

"We'll keep looking." Roxie sighed heavily. She wanted to ride her sled down the slope again.

"I want to go down again!" Donna grabbed Hannah's saucer and ran into line. "Let's go now. Please?"

Hannah looked at the Best Friends, and they shrugged. She turned back to Donna, who looked like she was ready to explode with excitement. "I guess it's all right."

Suddenly Donna dashed out of line and pushed in at the front of the line at the edge of the hill.

"Hey!" Hannah raced after Donna, but it was too late to stop her.

Donna dropped down on Hannah's saucer

and shot down the hill, twirling in circles most of the way to the bottom.

"I can't believe her!" Chelsea cried.

"What a little brat!" Roxie stared down the hill.

"She's almost at the bottom." Kathy shook her head. "What's wrong with her anyway?"

"I have to get my sled back." Hannah turned to go after Donna, and Eli was standing right there! Hannah's pulse leaped, and she almost sank to the snow.

"I'll get your sled," Eli said with a determined look on his face.

"You will?" Hannah's heart stood still. She glanced around for Alyson, but she wasn't in sight.

Eli flopped stomach-first onto his sled and shot down the hill.

Her eyes wide, Hannah clasped her hands and watched Eli zoom to the bottom. He jumped off his sled, looked around for Donna, then ran toward her.

"I hope he brings her back up here," Chelsea said, sounding worried. "We still have to help her find her sister."

Hannah heard the Best Friends talking beside her, but all her attention was on Eli. He'd come to her rescue! Could that mean he still liked her even though she wasn't allowed to date yet?

"Let's go down!" Chelsea nudged Hannah. "Ride with me."

Hannah squeezed onto Chelsea's sled with her, and they shot down the hill at breakneck speed. Hannah pressed her face against Chelsea's back to block the cold wind whistling past. At the bottom of the hill the sled finally stopped near Eli and Donna. He was holding Donna's arm with one hand and Hannah's saucer with the other. His own sled sat at his feet.

"I got her." Eli looked and sounded proud of himself.

"Thank you!" Smiling, Hannah almost melted into the snow.

Donna squirmed and kicked but couldn't break free. "Let me go right now before I call the cops!"

"Stop it, Donna Workman!" Hannah shook her finger at Donna. "You took my sled!"

Donna stopped struggling and hung her head. "I only wanted to ride down by myself. I don't have a sled."

Eli shook Donna's arm. "Why didn't you say so? Hannah's real nice. She would've let you take a turn on hers."

With stars in her eyes, Hannah smiled at Eli. He thought she was nice!

Eli smiled at Hannah. "What shall I do with this girl?"

Hannah shrugged. How could she think of Donna at a glorious time like this? A sharp elbow from Chelsea woke Hannah up, and she said, "We're trying to help her find her sister Susan."

Eli frowned down at Donna. "Is Susan here?"

Donna hunched her shoulders until her head was almost lost between the bulky shoulders of her jacket.

Eli looked closer at Donna. "Is her name Susan Workman?"

Donna nodded.

"Do you know her?" Roxie asked in surprise.

He nodded. "She's in my English class. A couple of weeks ago she broke her leg, and she's on crutches. She wouldn't be here."

Hannah stared at Donna in shock. "Why on earth did you lie to us?"

Donna lifted her head, and fire shot from her eyes. "I wanted to come sledding today, but I didn't have a sled! So I came anyway!"

Kathy frowned. "Did you walk?"

"Sure. I don't live very far away."

Hannah knew it was at least a half a mile to the nearest house. Mom would never let the twins walk that far alone. "Did you tell your family you were coming here today?"

Donna shrugged again. "Why should I?"

Hannah glanced at the Best Friends. She knew they were thinking the same thing she was—nobody at Donna's house cared where she was. Hannah knelt beside Donna. "You can use my sled for five more times down the hill, then I'll take it back."

Chelsea patted her sled. "After that, you can use my sled."

"Then mine," Kathy said, and Roxie said the same thing.

Eli laughed as he let go of Donna. "You can even use mine if you're not too tired then."

Donna looked at Eli and the Best Friends as if she didn't believe a word they said.

Hannah took her sled from Eli and held it out to Donna. "When you go down five times, find me and return my sled, then get Chelsea's."

"I will." Donna grabbed Hannah's saucer and started to run, then turned back. Her eyes glowed, and her cheeks were rosy. "Thank you!" She turned back and raced for the trail that led up to the top of the hill.

Smiling, Hannah watched Donna until she was lost in the crowd trudging up the hill. Hannah turned back. Alyson was walking toward them, her eyes on Eli. Hannah's heart sank. She wanted to grab Eli's arm and run up the hill with him and away from Alyson.

"Eli!" Alyson stopped beside Eli and smiled at him as if he were the love of her life. "Are you ready to go back up yet?"

Eli cleared his throat. "Hannah and I are going up, and we'll ride back down on my sled."

Hannah bit back a cry. She saw the anguish on Alyson's face, and she actually felt sorry for her, but not sorry enough to refuse a ride with Eli.

"Ready, Hannah?" Eli smiled and held out his hand.

"Ready." Hannah took his hand and walked toward the path leading up to the top of the hill.

9

Donna Workman

Hannah zoomed down the hill with Eli behind her on the sled and his arms around her to hold the rope. Her heart thudded so loud she was sure he could hear it even over the *swoosh* of the sled on the snow. Her whole mind was on Eli, and she didn't notice when the sled stopped. She felt him move, and she turned her head, then flushed. They were at the bottom of the hill with Alyson nearby. Hannah jumped up, flustered. What would Eli do now?

He smiled at Hannah. "That was fun. See you later."

Unable to speak, she nodded. Blood roared in her ears as Eli and Alyson walked away, talking and laughing. Alyson looked back and stuck her tongue out at Hannah. Hannah turned quickly away and blinked hard to keep from crying.

Laughing, Donna ran up to Hannah. "Want to ride down with me this time?"

"You go ahead. I'll rest for a while."

"Is something wrong? You look like you're going to cry."

"I'll be all right."

"You sure? I'll stay right here with you if you're not."

Hannah smiled. "That's nice of you, but you go ahead and have fun before you have to go home."

Donna shook her head. "It don't matter when I go home."

"Make sure you go back before dark though."

"I will." Donna ran off, Hannah's saucer-sled bouncing against her leg.

Hannah slowly walked around several kids to the concrete benches at the edge of the sledding area. She sat down and pulled off her knit cap. Her hair crackled with static electricity. The cold air felt good against her head. Sounds of people having fun drifted around her. She rubbed her cheeks and wrinkled her nose at the smell of her soggy mittens.

The Best Friends ran up and sat with Hannah. They were breathless from sliding down the hill.

Chelsea caught her breath and said, "Pete

Decker says we can ride on his toboggan next time down. Want to, Hannah?"

She could see that the others, even Roxie, were excited about it, so she agreed. It would help take her mind off Eli and Alyson.

Several minutes later the Best Friends stood beside Pete while he told each one where to ride. Hannah said she didn't want to be first and have snow fly into her face.

"This should be great!"

Hannah froze at the sudden sound of Alyson's voice. Slowly Hannah turned and saw Alyson and Eli standing next to the toboggan. Eli smiled at her, but Alyson scowled. Hannah wanted to run away, but Chelsea and Kathy stepped closer beside her and Roxie at her back. She couldn't run away!

"I'll sit up front," Pete said. "Eli, you take the back. This is a six man toboggan, but we'll squeeze on seven of us."

Hannah wanted to say she'd stay behind, but she knew the Best Friends wouldn't let her.

Roxie climbed on behind Pete and in front of Kathy, Chelsea, and Hannah. Alyson sat between Hannah and Eli. Hannah forced back a groan as she leaned her head on Chelsea's back.

Just then Alyson pulled Hannah's hair hard.

"You'll be sorry for butting in with me and Eli," Alyson whispered for Hannah's ears alone.

Shivering, Hannah didn't know what to say or do. Her head hurt from Alyson pulling her hair. Should she jump off? There was still time.

Suddenly Chelsea jumped off and motioned for Hannah to slide forward.

Relieved, Hannah moved close to Kathy while Chelsea sat behind Hannah.

"Ready! Go!" Eli shouted.

The toboggan started slow, then built up speed. Hannah kept her face against Kathy's back and her hands on Kathy's waist. Hannah relaxed, once again thankful for the Best Friends, especially Chelsea who clung tightly to her.

Hannah lifted her head a little and felt snow sting her face and wind whip past her. The ride seemed to go on and on, then suddenly was over. Laughing, Hannah jumped to her feet. Thanks to Chelsea, she'd had fun on the daring toboggan ride! Just as she turned to thank Chelsea, a snowball struck her in the face. She cried out and fell backwards into the snow. Red with embarrassment, she scrambled to her feet.

Looking concerned, Chelsea reached for Hannah. "What happened?"

Hannah brushed snow off her face and looked around at Alyson. She was innocently talking to Eli. She glanced at Hannah with a smirk on her face, then caught Eli's hand and led him away.

"I'll get her yet," Hannah whispered angrily.

Kathy caught Hannah's arm. "No . . . No, you won't."

Hannah pushed her anger away and smiled. Sometimes it was very hard to be like Jesus. "No . . . I won't. Let's go check on Donna."

Several minutes later the Best Friends stood on top of the hill where they'd left their sleds to go on the toboggan ride. Hannah couldn't see Donna anywhere.

"I hope Donna didn't take my sled and go home." Hannah pushed her hands into her pockets as she again looked over the crowd for Donna Workman. It would be terrible if Donna took the sled home! It really belonged to Lena. The twins had their own. Heather Robbins had come to play with the twins a couple of weeks ago and had left Hannah's plastic saucer out in the yard. When Hannah started to break it loose from the icy ground, it had split, so she'd used Lena's saucer today.

Just then Hannah spotted Donna sitting beside the first line. She was crying, and she didn't have Hannah's sled. "Oh, no. She's crying again."

The Best Friends ran to Donna and knelt around her. "What's wrong?" Hannah asked.

Donna's lip quivered as she looked sadly at Hannah. "Some bratty boy took your sled from me. I tried to take it away from him, but he was too strong."

Hannah angrily looked around. "Where is he now?"

"Somewhere."

"Did he just slide down?"

Donna shrugged. She peered down the hill, then pointed excitedly. "That's him! He's got on a blue snowmobile suit. See him? He has your red saucer!"

Hannah and the others looked where Donna was pointing and finally picked the boy out of the crowd.

Suddenly Donna grabbed Roxie's sled. "I'll get him!" She jumped ahead of the girl getting ready to go down and shot down the hill.

Hannah gasped, then turned to the girl who was waiting to go down. "Could I please go next? I have to help that little girl!"

"Sure, go ahead."

"Thanks!" Hannah seized Chelsea's sled and whizzed down the hill. Before the sled stopped she jumped off, caught the sled before it got away, then raced toward Donna, who was trying to take the sled away from the boy she'd identified.

Suddenly Donna punched the boy in the nose. "Don't you never take my sled again!"

The boy held his nose and started to cry. "You gave me a bloody nose!"

"You stole my sled!" Donna looked ready to punch the boy again.

"Donna!" Hannah caught Donna's arm in time to stop her.

Donna held the saucer close to her. Roxie's sled lay at her feet. She laughed triumphantly. "I got it back!"

Smiling, Hannah patted Donna's back, then bent down to the boy. He was probably eight years old. He had a big rip in his snowmobile suit. "I'm Hannah. What's your name?"

"Randy Marsh. She gave me a bloody nose!"

Hannah pulled a tissue from her pocket and gave it to Randy. While he dabbed at his nose she said, "Why'd you take the sled from Donna?"

He shrugged.

"He don't have a sled." Donna stepped closer to him. "He thought he could take mine! Well, he can't!"

Randy struggled hard to keep from crying.

Hannah felt sorry for him. She turned to Donna. "Did I let you use my sled because you didn't have one?"

Donna reluctantly nodded.

"Don't you think you could share it with Randy since he doesn't have a sled?"

Donna shook her head. "I don't want to share!"

"Randy feels sad because he can't have fun like kids with sleds. I would like to see him smile and be happy."

Donna shook her head hard. "Not me!"

Hannah could see she wasn't going to change Donna's mind. Hannah handed Randy Roxie's sled. "You can use this for three times down, then give it back to me."

He looked at her as if she were weird. "You think I'd give it back if I took it? No way! I'd take it home."

"Why?"

"You're dumb to think I wouldn't!" Randy turned and raced away.

Donna patted Hannah's arm. "Don't feel bad because he wouldn't use the sled. He never has nobody be nice to him."

"Do you know him?"

"I've seen him at school."

"I thought you didn't know him."

Donna shrugged. "I didn't know his name, but I saw him grab food in the lunchroom from other kids."

"I feel sorry for him."

"Not me!" Donna started away, then turned back. "I guess I feel a little sorry for him. He should've used the sled so he could have fun."

Hannah laughed. "He should've. You go ahead. Are you sure you're not tired yet?"

"I'm tired, but I'm not stopping until I have to." Donna giggled and ran toward the end of the hill. Then she dashed back. "I was gonna steal your sled, but I won't now."

"Thank you." Hannah hugged Donna.

"Did you come on that church bus today?"

"Yes."

Donna was quiet a long time. "I don't go to church."

"You're welcome to come to ours." Hannah told Donna where it was. "If you need a ride, you can call the church and someone will pick you up."

"Okay." Donna grinned and ran off, clutching the saucer-sled to her.

Hannah smiled as she picked up Roxie's and Chelsea's sleds. Before she could move, Roxie and Kathy ran up to her.

"Chelsea's waiting on top for us," Roxie said, pointing to the top of the hill where Chelsea was waving at them.

Hannah waved, then told the girls what had

happened as they walked to the end of the hill. "Not even Alyson could make me feel bad now."

"Good, because here she comes," Roxie whispered.

Hannah frowned. "Where's Eli?"

Roxie giggled. "Maybe he dumped her."

Kathy jabbed Roxie in the arm. "That's not very nice."

Hannah and the girls kept walking. They came face to face with Alyson and started to go around her when she stopped them.

Alyson looked close to tears. "Have you seen Eli?"

"Not since the toboggan ride," Roxie said. "Why?"

Hannah wanted to run as far away from Alyson as she could get, but she didn't move.

Alyson bit her lip. "I think he left me."

Hannah's heart soared. "Oh?"

Alyson rubbed her hands nervously up and down her yellow jacket sleeves. "I don't know how I'll get home if he left without me."

Scowling, Roxie stepped right up to Alyson. "My brother would never leave his date behind, even if he had a fight with her!"

Alyson flushed. "Well . . . it wasn't actually a date."

Hannah stood totally still. Not a date? She couldn't find her voice to ask what it was.

Kathy tipped her head and studied Alyson. "What actually was it?"

Her face white, Alyson twisted the toe of her boot in the snow as people walked around them to get to the path. "I told him I needed a ride, and he gave me one."

Hannah bit back a happy shout. "Eli wouldn't leave you behind if he knew you needed a ride."

"How do you know?" Alyson asked coldly.

"Because I know Eli." Hannah turned to Roxie. "Am I right?"

Roxie nodded. "My brother would never leave you behind! He must be here somewhere."

"Want us to help you find him?" Hannah asked.

Alyson fell back a step. "Why?"

"Because you need help," Kathy said impatiently. "Come on."

Alyson looked bewildered. "I don't understand you girls at all!"

"Jesus says to be kind to each other," Roxie said.

"And to love each other." Kathy patted Alyson's arm. "Let us help you."

"We'll find Eli." Smiling, Hannah walked toward the path. She'd find Eli and ask if he'd slide down the hill with her again. This time she'd enjoy the ride.

10

Questions

Hannah practically floated across the snowy hill as they looked for Eli in the brilliantly colored crowd of people. He had not brought Alyson as his date! What wonderfully magnificent news!

"There he is!" Roxie pointed ahead at Eli, standing with a group of boys from his class.

Hannah's heart flip-flopped. Oh, but Eli was handsome! He was the best-looking, the nicest, and the smartest boy in the group! In the entire universe! Just then he looked at her, and she couldn't breathe. Then the other boys looked at her too. She flushed. Had Eli told them he liked her? She suddenly felt almost too weak to keep walking. The shouts and laughter faded in the background as her mind filled with thoughts of Eli.

Alyson pulled back, and the Best Friends

stopped with her. "I don't want to talk to Eli when he's with those boys."

Jerked back to her surroundings, Hannah questioningly frowned at Alyson. "How come?"

"They make me feel funny—like they're laughing at me or something." Alyson shuddered. "I don't think they're very nice."

Roxie glanced at the group of boys, then back at Alyson. "I've heard Eli talk about them. He doesn't think they're nice either. They're always teasing him and daring him to do things."

"Maybe he needs to be rescued from them," Hannah whispered as she pictured herself leaping to save Eli from a fate worse than death.

Chelsea tapped her sled. "Or maybe we should go sledding like we came to do. You can ride with me, Hannah."

Kathy held her sled out toward Alyson. "You can ride with me if you want."

Alyson looked questioningly toward Eli. "As long as he won't leave me behind."

"He won't," Roxie said impatiently. "Let's go down again before we have to get on the bus."

The others agreed, but Hannah had a fantastic plan. She waited until the others stood in the short line waiting to go down, then whispered to Chelsea, "Go on without me. I'll ride down with Eli."

Chelsea's eyes widened. "Are you going to ask him with those boys hanging around him?"

"Sure." Hannah sounded more confident than she felt. "Don't worry about me."

"Okay." Chelsea bit her lip. "Are you sure?"

Hannah nodded, then laughed softly. "He likes me, Chel. He asked me to come with him today. Remember?"

"You're right." Chelsea giggled and patted her heart in quick, little pats. "I wish Brody was here—I'd see if he'd ride down with me." Brody was Kathy's foster brother, and Chelsea had liked him for the last several weeks. Brody and Kathy's brother Duke were playing their guitars and singing at a birthday party along with Stacia King, the black girl who lived with her grandparents at The Ravines.

Hannah slowly walked toward Eli and the boys. They looked her way again and she hesitated, her stomach fluttering nervously. Maybe this wasn't such a good idea after all.

As she hesitated Eli stepped forward, his sled in his hand. "Hi, Hannah."

"Hi." She could barely speak. Her jacket felt too hot.

The boys laughed. One said, "So this is Hannah Shigwam."

Eli frowned back at the boys, and they laughed harder.

Hannah suddenly wished she'd gone with Chelsea.

"Did you want something?" Eli smiled hesitantly.

She nodded. "I thought . . . we could ride down together again. That is, if you want."

"Sure. Okay." Eli glanced around. "There's a short line over there. Let's go."

Hannah fell into step beside Eli. She didn't say anything until they were almost at the short line. "Were those boys your friends?"

"They're in my English class."

"Why'd they know who I was?"

Eli flushed. "It doesn't matter."

Hannah looked closely at him. He looked upset. "Is something wrong?"

"Let's slide down. Then we'll talk."

Hannah stiffened. "What about?"

"Things. Wait'll we go down."

Hannah stepped ahead with Eli as the line moved forward. There were only two boys ahead of them. Hannah moved restlessly from one booted foot to the other. She ignored the screams floating up the hill and the laughter all around her. "Why can't you tell me now?"

Eli cleared his throat. "Please wait, Hannah. Okay?"

She saw his discomfort, and she smiled. Anything he said was fine with her. "Okay." What was making him so uneasy?

Finally it was their turn to go down. Hannah shivered in delight as Eli put his arms around her to hold the rope. The pulse-pounding excitement of sledding down the steep hill was nothing compared to the pulse-pounding excitement of being close to Eli. She never wanted to reach the bottom of the hill. Maybe he'd want to go down again and again with her. She'd give him a chance to ask. Or maybe she'd ask him. What did it matter how those boys knew her. She didn't need any answers from Eli.

At the bottom of the hill Eli picked up his sled and headed for a cement bench.

Her eyes sparkling, Hannah ran in front of him and stopped him. "Let's go back up again! We don't need to talk now."

Eli looked very stern. "Yes, we do." He stepped around her and dropped down on the bench, letting his sled fall to the ground.

Hannah's stomach knotted. What was wrong with Eli? She didn't know if she wanted to have this talk with him. Anxiously she looked around for the Best Friends. She couldn't see them among the crowd.

"Sit down, Hannah." Eli unzipped his jacket. "It's hot all at once."

Hannah looked closely at him. He was definitely nervous! What was he going to say to her? Weakly she sank to the bench beside him.

Eli took a deep breath. "You wanted to know why those boys knew your name."

"It doesn't matter," Hannah said quickly. She felt she had to stop Eli, but she didn't know why.

"I have to tell you! I have to!" Eli dabbed his face with his gloved hand.

Hannah bit her lip. What was wrong with him?

He took a deep breath. "We have a special English assignment."

Hannah let out her breath in one *whoosh*. Why had she been so worried?

"We have to interview someone . . . different."

"Different?"

"Not the same . . . race as ourselves."

Hannah frowned.

"So I decided to interview you because you're Native American."

Hannah stiffened. Was that why he'd been paying so much attention to her? "When did you learn about the assignment?"

"A few weeks ago."

"When is it due?"

"Next Friday."

Tears stung the backs of Hannah's eyes, but she wouldn't let them fall. She didn't want to ask him, but she had to know. "Did you . . . ask me to come here with you today so you could do your assignment without me knowing what you were doing?"

Looking guilty, Eli nodded.

Hannah felt like her heart had just stopped beating. She couldn't move or speak.

"Are you mad at me?"

She thought to herself, *Mad? Hurt, maybe. Devastated, for sure.* Finally she whispered, "Why couldn't you just ask me?"

"I thought you'd be mad at me. Roxie said you were—well, sensitive about being Ottawa Indian."

Hannah couldn't speak.

"I'm real sorry, Hannah. I didn't want to make you feel bad. Honest."

"I know," she whispered. She wanted to run from him, but her legs felt too weak to hold her.

"Can I ask you some questions now?"

Hannah shrugged.

"Do you ever wish you were white?"

Hannah moved her head up and down slightly.

She hated to admit she felt that way, but it was the truth. If she were white, she wouldn't be feeling this awful pain right now or be answering his terrible questions.

"Do you feel you're equal to whites?"

She lifted pain-filled eyes to Eli. "That's an awful question to ask."

"I know, but the teacher made up the list of questions."

"Tell your teacher that all men are created equal."

Eli moved restlessly. "He said we'd get that answer and that we're not to accept it."

Hannah thought for a moment or two, then asked, "Do you feel you're equal to Ottawas?"

Eli flushed. "Don't, Hannah."

"That's a fair question. Well? Do you?"

"I don't want to answer."

Hannah brushed at her eyes. "I already know the answer! Roxie told me. You and your family think you're better than Ottawas!"

Eli ducked his head. "I'm sorry."

Hannah's eyes flashed. "Why didn't you pick on someone else for this assignment? Why me?"

"Because I thought I could talk to you without hurting your feelings."

"You were wrong!"

"Maybe it's the questions."

"Or the way you approached me." Hannah locked her hands together in her lap. "Why couldn't you just walk up to me, tell me about the assignment, and ask me the questions?"

"I wish I had."

"So do I." Just then Hannah spotted the Best Friends. She jumped up. "I gotta go!" She ran off before Eli could stop her. She reached the Best Friends and struggled to hold back the tears of agony. Eli didn't like her for a girlfriend like she'd thought! She'd been his English assignment!

Chelsea gripped Hannah's arm and peered into her face. "What's wrong?"

"Tell us!" Roxie and Kathy said together.

"I can't," Hannah whispered. "Not here."

"It's Eli, isn't it?" Roxie stamped her foot angrily. "What did he do to you?"

"Is it time to leave yet?" Hannah looked at her watch, willing it to be time. She couldn't stay another minute or answer another question.

"They're loading the bus now." Kathy patted Hannah's arm. "We were just coming to get you."

"I got your sled from Donna." Chelsea held up the red saucer. "So we're almost ready to go."

"Good!"

"Alyson is riding with Eli like she planned," Roxie said softly. "Is that what's bothering you so much?"

Hannah shook her head.

"We want to ask Eli to take Donna home so she doesn't have to walk." Chelsea cleared her throat. "Will you come with us to ask him?"

Hannah jumped back. "No! I'll wait in the bus."

"Oh my," Roxie whispered. "Eli really did hurt you, didn't he?"

Hannah nodded.

Roxie tugged Kathy's arm. "We'll talk to Eli and let Chelsea and Hannah go to the bus."

Kathy agreed and walked away with Roxie.

Chelsea slipped her arm through Hannah's. "Don't you let anybody, not even Eli Shoulders, make you sad! You hear me?"

Hannah nodded. She heard all right, but it didn't do any good. Eli had destroyed her. She might never be happy again.

11

The Special Meeting

Hannah walked toward the exit of the church. She'd barely made it through Sunday school and church without bursting into tears. Now if she could just get to the station wagon before anyone stopped to talk to her, she'd be all right. In the station wagon nobody would be there to see her cry—until the family came. But it always took them a long time to get the baby from the nursery and the girls from children's church.

Suddenly Donna Workman ran down the tiled hall and flung herself at Hannah. "I didn't think you were here!"

Hannah hugged Donna and managed to smile. "Hi. I'm glad to see you found a ride this morning."

"Eli Shoulders picked me up."

Hannah gasped.

"He took me home after I went sledding yesterday, and he said he'd bring me to church this morning." Donna giggled and flipped back her dark hair. "I like Sunday school. Don't you?"

Hannah nodded.

"I want to come to Sunday school from now on. Susan might too."

"That's nice."

Just then Grandma Agatha walked up, leaning heavily on her cane. "Hello, Hannah."

"Hi." Hannah smiled. "Grandma Agatha, this is my new friend Donna Workman. She lives just outside of town near where we went sledding yesterday."

"Hello, Donna." Grandma Agatha patted Donna's arm.

Donna's eyes widened. "I know who you are—the grandma who tells stories! I heard some girls talking about you!"

Grandma Agatha smiled and looked pleased. "I guess I'm famous."

"Tell me a story, will you?" Donna clung to Grandma Agatha's hand. "I don't have a grandma. Did you know that? I don't have a sled or a grandma."

As Grandma Agatha looked down at Donna clinging to her, Hannah saw love on the old woman's face where only a few days ago there'd been despair and anger.

"Suppose I come see you this afternoon. I could tell you a story and be your grandma for the afternoon."

"Okay!" Donna jumped up and down. She grabbed Hannah's hand. "Will you come with her? I want to show Susan that you're real and that you did let me use your sled. She thinks I probably stole it. I said I didn't, but she didn't believe me. Will you come too, Hannah?"

"Of course she will," Grandma Agatha said, patting Donna's shoulder.

Hannah didn't have the heart to say differently. She didn't want to go! She wanted to hide in her room away from everybody! She hadn't been able to bring herself to tell the Best Friends what had happened. Maybe she could after school tomorrow. She'd see how she felt then.

After Sunday dinner Hannah zipped her jacket as she walked slowly to the Griggs house to meet Grandma Agatha as she'd agreed. She squinted in the bright sun that made the snow sparkle. It would be easier to go with Grandma Agatha than to tell the Best Friends she couldn't talk to them yet. Donna and Grandma Agatha would help take her mind off Eli.

Just then the door opened, and Grandma Agatha walked out. She looked rested and happy. Her navy-blue wool coat reached to the tops of her navy-blue leather boots. "Hello, Hannah! I'm glad you're right on time."

Hannah smiled. "It's so nice of you to go see Donna. I feel sorry for her. She doesn't seem to have anyone who cares about her."

"That's what Eli said."

Hannah froze. "Eli?"

"Yes. I talked to him right after church." Grandma Agatha looked past Hannah. "Here he comes now. He's driving us to Donna's."

Hannah looked wildly around. Could she hide in the igloo? How could she get out of going with Grandma Agatha?

"What's wrong, Hannah?" Grandma Agatha asked in concern.

Before Hannah could answer, Eli stopped his car at the curb and ran to assist Grandma Agatha.

"Hello, Grandma Agatha." Eli smiled, then glanced at Hannah. "Hi."

Hannah forced out a weak hello as she followed them to the car. It belonged to Eli's dad, but Eli was allowed to drive it until he saved enough money to buy a car of his own.

"I hope the sun doesn't melt the igloo," Eli said as he held the door open for Grandma Agatha.

Hannah opened the back door for herself and slid in. The car smelled like spearmint chewing gum. She looked at the igloo. Was the sun really warm enough to melt it, or was Eli only making conversation? As he closed Grandma Agatha's door and ran around the front of the car, Hannah said, "Will the igloo melt?"

"Reece went out last night when the temperature dipped down to zero and poured water over it. It froze solid, so this sun won't melt it. Not yet anyway."

"Good!" Hannah sat back in relief. For some reason she didn't want the igloo to melt. She knew it had to someday, but she wanted it to stay as long as possible.

Eli pulled away from the curb while Grandma Agatha asked him about school.

Hannah held her breath. He didn't say anything about his assignment, and she slowly let out her breath. She listened to Eli and Grandma Agatha without saying a word.

As Eli pulled into Donna's driveway and stopped outside the garage, Grandma Agatha glanced back at Hannah. "You're awfully quiet back there. Is anything wrong?"

"She's upset with me," Eli said in a strained voice.

Hannah flushed painfully.

"I'm sorry to hear that. I'm sure you'll get it settled. Hannah's not one to hold a grudge."

Hannah slipped out of the car without answering. She'd never thought she'd be unforgiving, but that was before yesterday. She started toward the one-story frame house painted blue. A rose trellis, bare for the winter, stood beside the front steps leading up to the door.

The door opened, and Donna ran out without a coat. Her dark hair flowed loose over her shoulders. She wore the same jeans and pink sweater she'd worn to church. "You came! You came!" She flung her arms around Hannah and hugged her tight. "I told Susan you'd come, but she didn't think you would."

Hannah patted Donna's shoulder before the little girl raced to hug Grandma Agatha and Eli.

"Mom and Dad aren't home. But I am, and Susan is." Donna held Grandma Agatha's hand and walked up the sidewalk to the door that still stood open.

Grandma Agatha hesitated at the door. "Maybe we should come another day."

"No!" Donna shook her head hard. "You said you'd come tell me a story today! You said so!"

Grandma Agatha laughed softly. "So I did."

Hannah hung back while Donna led Grandma Agatha inside.

"I am sorry," Eli said softly with his head down close to Hannah's.

Her heart jerked. "Please don't say anything," she said hoarsely. She hurried inside before he could say more. The front door opened directly into a living room painted white. It had a flowered sofa and chairs and a portable TV sitting on a stand with a VCR on a shelf beside a tape rewinder. Music drifted out from a room down the narrow hall.

Donna caught Hannah's hand and smiled up at her. "Susan wants you to go to her room to see her, so just walk right down that hall. Her door's open."

Feeling awkward, Hannah walked slowly to the room with the music. She heard the words of the song and frowned. It was a song about death and despair and what a waste life was. She hesitated at the doorway. The music surrounded her and seemed to weight her down.

"Come in," Susan called from inside the room.

Hannah slowly stepped inside. A poster with a skull superimposed over a girl dressed in black hung beside the bed and seemed to overwhelm the room. Hannah shivered.

Dressed in an oversized black T-shirt, Susan sat on her bed, her brown eyes filled with sadness, her cast-covered leg stretched out over the covers. "You must be Hannah."

"Yes." Hannah forced a smile. "I'm sorry about your broken leg."

"Yeah, me too." Susan waved toward a chair next to a small desk cluttered with papers and books. "Take off your coat and sit down. I wanted to see if you were real or not."

Hannah frowned slightly as she draped her jacket over the back of the wooden chair. "Real?"

"Donna told me about you letting her use your sled. I said nobody was that nice." Susan hooked her straight brown hair over her ears. "Donna said *you* are."

"I like to help others." Hannah perched on the edge of the chair. She glanced toward the tape player on the stand beside the bed. She wanted to click the cassette tape out of the player and toss it in the wastebasket.

"Do you like my music?"

Hannah shook her head. "It's too gloomy for me."

"I know. But that's why I like it." Susan rubbed her hands up and down her arms. "Do you ever think about death?"

"Some."

"It intrigues me. Does it scare you?"

"A little, but I know when I die I'll go to Heaven to be with Jesus."

Susan's eyes widened. "Or go to Hell—and doom and despair."

"No!" Hannah shook her head hard. "Jesus is my personal Lord and Savior. When I die, I will go to Heaven. The Bible says so, and it's God's Word!"

Susan leaned forward slightly. "You sound very sure of yourself."

"I am."

Susan twisted a strand of hair around her finger. "I think about dying—sinking away into nothing. I think of walking in Hell and screaming in torment just like the song says. It sounds so poetic—so awesome!"

Hannah leaped up and clicked off the terrible music. "It isn't poetic or awesome! And you don't have to go there and suffer the torment. You have a choice." Hannah smiled at Susan. "You don't even have to suffer torment right now like that song says! You can be happy! You can have peace in your heart . . . and hope."

Hope flashed in Susan's eyes, then was gone. She shook her head. "The world is doomed. It's getting worse and worse and will explode. Then where will we be? Why live knowing that's all I have to look forward to?"

Hannah's head whirled. She'd never faced such despair before. How she wished the Best Friends were there with her to help her talk to Susan. They weren't there, but Jesus was! Silently she prayed for the right words to speak to help Susan. "Look at me, Susan!" Hannah tapped her chest. "It doesn't matter if the whole world falls down around me since I know Jesus. He causes me to be victorious in all things. He makes me more than a conqueror! Jesus makes life worth living for me. And He will do the same for you if you let Him. That's the truth, Susan!"

"Nobody ever told me that." Susan's eyes were big and round. "My friends feel the same as I do. They know life is hopeless."

"They're wrong! You're wrong! God loves you, and He wants the very best for you."

Susan brushed a tear off her eyelashes. "Why did you care if Donna had fun or not yesterday?"

"I just did. The Bible says God's love is shed abroad in my heart by the Holy Spirit."

"What does God care about a sled ride for Donna?"

"He loves her and wants her to be happy."

Susan rolled her eyes. "Happy! Who's happy in this world?"

"People who trust in God and have asked

Him to forgive them for the wrong things they've done."

"Want to know how I broke my leg?"

Hannah nodded.

"I had an accident. I guess maybe it was on purpose. I didn't think I could go on living anymore."

Hannah's stomach lurched. "I . . . But why?"

"To end my misery."

"It wouldn't end your misery. Don't you understand that? Without Jesus you'd live in misery forever."

"So?"

"So you don't have to, Susan. You can be full of joy and peace and love. I'm telling you the truth."

Tears rolled down Susan's cheeks. "When Donna told me about your sled, I knew you could help me."

Hannah stepped close to the bed and caught Susan's hand in hers. "I can show you the way to Jesus."

"That's what I want." Susan's voice came out in a whisper as she clung to Hannah's hand.

Hannah took a deep breath and told Susan about Jesus dying on the cross for her, then being raised from the dead to live in Heaven forever. "He loves you, Susan. He knows who you are and what you want. Accept Him as your personal Savior, ask Him to forgive you, and He'll fill your heart with love instead of despair." Hannah bowed her head and prayed for Susan, then helped her ask Jesus to be her Lord and Savior.

Susan wiped away her tears and blew her nose. "I'm so glad you came today!"

"Me too." Hannah wiped away her tears with a tissue from Susan's box. "Now that Jesus is your Savior, you must choose between listening to the kind of music that'll destroy you or music that tells you of God's love and what He wants to do for you."

Susan clicked out the tape and tossed it into the wastebasket. "Will you take down the poster and throw it away too? It gives me nightmares. Rip it up!"

Hannah gladly took down the poster, folded it, and ripped it into several pieces, then pushed it into the wastebasket. The room felt different already. "Do you have a Bible, Susan?"

She nodded. "It's in my bottom desk drawer way at the back. I got it for Christmas when I was ten. I threw it away a lot of times, but every time I'd pull it back out."

Hannah found the Bible, opened it to the Gospel of John, and laid it beside Susan. "Start reading John first, then read the rest of the New

Testament. Read every single day, and think about what you read. Pray every day too. Praying is just having a conversation with God."

Susan pressed the open Bible against her cheek, and her face glowed. Not even the black shirt could mar her radiance. "Thank you, Hannah! I won't forget what you've done for me . . . And for Donna."

"I'm sure glad I could help." Hannah picked up Susan's crutches. "Want to meet Grandma Agatha?"

Smiling, Susan nodded and reached for her crutches.

Hannah's heart soared as she walked to the living room with Susan.

Eli jumped up and helped Susan to a chair as Grandma Agatha greeted the girl on crutches.

Hannah ducked her head and sat as far away from Eli as she could get.

12

Best Friends Together

Sighing, Hannah hung her jacket in the closet. Part of her was still elated over Susan accepting Jesus as her Savior, and part of her was in the depths of despair over Eli.

Hannah hesitated in the hall. The house seemed unusually quiet. Maybe everybody was taking a Sunday afternoon nap. That was unheard of for the twins and Lena. They thought a nap was the worst torture in the world—worse than eating liver and onions.

Slowly Hannah walked downstairs to the basement bedroom she shared with the twins and Lena. She heard a noise and sighed. They were there, and she wouldn't have a chance to be alone.

Just as Hannah reached the bottom step, the Best Friends stepped into sight. Gasping, Hannah felt the color drain from her face. She wasn't ready for them. "I didn't know you girls were here."

"We knew you needed us." Chelsea grinned as she slipped her arm through Hannah's.

Roxie nodded. "We asked your dad if we could wait down here for you."

"Your mom and dad knew something was bothering you, so they were glad for our help." Kathy laughed softly. "So, here we are."

Hannah wasn't ready to talk, so she forced a bright smile. "Wait'll you hear about Susan, Donna's sister!"

"Tell us!"

Hannah led the Best Friends to the fat cushions on the floor in the area where the twins had their play kitchen. Hannah sank to a cushion and waited for the girls to sit down too. Maybe if she kept them talking about Susan, Donna, and even Grandma Agatha, they wouldn't ask her about Eli.

Just thinking about Susan sent excitement bubbling inside Hannah again. She told the Best Friends about Susan's room and how depressed she was and how Hannah was able to tell her about Jesus. They talked about others they knew who were like Susan and how sad it was to watch them destroy themselves with bad songs and posters and even poems written just to glorify death.

After a while Hannah ran out of things to say.

She tried to think of something and couldn't. The Best Friends waited expectantly. She flushed and looked nervously around the basement they'd had fun turning into a bedroom/playroom. One wall was a closet with shelves and bars for hanging clothes on. Even with four girls sharing it, it wasn't full.

Chelsea touched Hannah's arm. "How can we help you if you don't talk to us about what's bothering you?"

"About Eli," Roxie said softly.

Hannah shook her head. "It's too embarrassing!"

Kathy pointed to herself, then the others. "Look, Hannah, we're your best friends. You don't need to be embarrassed with us. Remember?"

Hannah opened her mouth to say she didn't want to talk about Eli yet, but the entire story burst out instead.

"I can't believe him!" Roxie cried, throwing her hands into the air.

Chelsea shook her head. "I didn't think Eli would ever do anything like that."

"But just think how terrible *he* feels!" Kathy looked ready to cry.

Hannah bit her lip. "He did say he was sorry."

"I'm glad to hear that," Roxie said in great

relief. "It'll make it easier for me to forgive him and keep being friends with him." She'd been working hard to get to know him better so they could be friends as well as brother and sister.

Hannah looked down at her hands locked together in her lap.

Roxie frowned. "You are going to forgive him, aren't you, Hannah?"

"Of course she is." Smiling, Chelsea squeezed Hannah's arm. "Hannah is always the first to forgive anyone who does something bad to her."

"Not this time," Hannah whispered with her head down.

The Best Friends gasped, and then all talked at once. Finally Chelsea raised her hand. "Hold it! We can't all talk at the same time. And we are not going to make Hannah feel worse."

"Thank you." Hannah pulled her knees to her chin and wrapped her arms around her legs.

"But we are going to remind you that you have to forgive Eli because Jesus says to." Chelsea grinned at Hannah. "You know that as well as we do. In fact, you . . . you are the very girl who tells us when we try to forget."

The others laughed and nodded.

"She's right," Kathy said. "Remember when I wouldn't forgive Alyssa Carroll because she didn't want me to try out as a cheerleader?"

"I remember."

"I forgave her, didn't I?"

Hannah nodded.

Kathy giggled. "I sure didn't want to! But Jesus said to, and you reminded me of that."

"Me too," Roxie said at the same time Chelsea did.

Hannah listened to them and knew no matter how she felt, she had to obey what Jesus said and forgive Eli. She'd known it all along but had refused to consider it. Now, thanks to her friends, she couldn't put it off any longer. With a laugh she held out her hands. "Okay, okay, I forgive Eli." She didn't feel any better toward him, but she knew obedience to God's Word was what counted. As the girls all talked at once, she silently asked Jesus to forgive her for being disobedient.

Later Chelsea jumped up. "I'm ready for a game of Clue. Who else is?"

Hannah laughed happily. They knew it was her favorite game because she liked solving mysteries so much. She got the game from the closet and set it on the floor.

Just then the stair door opened, and Hannah's mom called, "Are you down there, Hannah?"

"Yes . . . With Chelsea, Roxie, and Kathy."

"Alyson's here to see you. I'll send her down."

Hannah groaned.

Kathy ran to meet Alyson. "We're just starting a game. Want to join in?"

Hannah didn't want Alyson to stay, but she couldn't be rude and tell her to leave.

Alyson's eyes were red-rimmed as if she'd been crying. She smiled hesitantly. "Hi. I didn't know you had company."

"That's all right."

Roxie tapped the Clue board. "Want to play with us?"

Alyson shook her head as she fingered the zipper on her yellow jacket. "Have you seen Brittany? I already asked your mom, and she said she hasn't."

Hannah shook her head. "Did you ask your grandma?"

"She's not home. She left again after she came back from seeing that girl Donna. I was watching Luann and Brittany for Mom and Dad." Alyson took a deep breath. "I was on the phone for a long time, and when I got off Brittany was gone. Luann was watching *Cinderella* on the VCR and didn't notice Brittany leave."

"Did you look in the igloo?" Roxie asked.

Alyson nodded.

Hannah frowned. "Did she go with your grandma?"

"I don't know where she went!" Alyson sounded close to tears.

"We'll help you look." Hannah quickly put the game away as the Best Friends slipped on their jackets.

"Thank you," Alyson whispered.

Hannah led the way upstairs, slipped on her jacket and boots, hurried outdoors, and stopped near the igloo. The sun was low in the sky, and the temperature had dropped. "Are you sure she's not hiding in the house?"

"She's not."

"Where's Luann?"

"Still watching the video."

Hannah gasped. "Alone? She's home all alone?"

Alyson flushed. "I have to find Brittany! What else could I do?"

"We'll look for Brittany." Hannah looked at the Best Friends to see if they agreed. They nodded, so she turned back to Alyson. "You stay with Luann."

Alyson swallowed hard. "I don't know how to thank you."

Hannah shrugged. "Do you have any idea where your grandma went?"

"No."

"She wouldn't walk by herself," Chelsea said. They all knew how hard it was for her to walk.

"Did anyone pick her up in a car?" Roxie looked intently at Alyson.

"I don't know."

"Who saw her last? Besides you, I mean." Kathy asked.

Alyson frowned in thought. "Eli and you, Hannah."

"We'll ask Eli if he knows where she went," Roxie said.

Hannah's blood froze. Could she face Eli again?

Alyson ran to her house while the Best Friends started across the street. Hannah couldn't budge. It was as if her boots had frozen to the snowy yard.

Chelsea looked back at Hannah, then ran to her side. "Come on! You can see him. You forgave him, remember?"

"I know." Hannah hesitated a second more, then ran with Chelsea to the others. They all reached Roxie's house at the same time. She led them through the back door. The smell of chili filled the hallway.

"Eli!" Roxie called.

He poked his head out of the kitchen and flushed when he saw Hannah. "What's up?"

Hannah's knees turned weak, but she didn't faint or run away.

Roxie explained why they were there. "Do you know where Grandma Agatha went after you dropped her off?"

"Sure. To the McCreas'."

Chelsea gasped. "*My* house?"

"Before I drove away from the Griggs house, Mike ran across the street and begged Grandma Agatha to come tell him a story. She said she had to go inside a minute but would go over right afterwards."

"Thanks, Eli!" Roxie waved and raced out the door.

Hannah followed, thankful she'd been able to look at Eli without anger or embarrassment.

In Chelsea's house they found Grandma Agatha in the living room telling a story about building a snow fort. Brittany was sitting beside Mike as if she belonged there. Chelsea's parents were listening and enjoying the story as much as the kids.

Quietly Chelsea led the way to the kitchen where she called Alyson to let her know Brittany was there. "We'll bring her home as soon as Grandma Agatha is finished with the story."

Hannah gazed out the kitchen window at the winter-bare bushes and trees. Would she ever be able to talk to Eli as if nothing had happened between them? Could she be friends with Alyson? Sometimes life was very hard!

Chelsea tugged Hannah's hair. "Smile, Hannah. We found Brittany, didn't we?"

Her eyes twinkling, Roxie stepped close to Hannah. "And you saw Eli without punching him in the nose for what he did to you."

Hannah giggled. She'd never punched anyone in the nose in her entire life.

Chelsea peeked into the refrigerator. "Anybody want apple juice or anything?"

Hannah was thankful for Chelsea's taking the attention off her. "I'll take some apple juice. Thanks."

Several minutes later Hannah told the Best Friends good-bye. Kathy rode her bike toward home as Hannah walked across the street with Brittany and Grandma Agatha.

"Alyson was worried about Brittany," Hannah said as they reached her friends' front door. Brittany ran inside, but Hannah and Grandma Agatha stayed on the front steps.

"I told her Brittany was going with me. I guess she didn't hear. Young people are like that sometimes—off in a world of their own. A bomb could burst beside them and they wouldn't hear it." Grandma Agatha laughed. "I suppose it was like that in my day too."

Hannah smiled. She couldn't imagine living in Grandma Agatha's day. "It was nice of you to tell stories to Donna and to Mike."

"I enjoyed it." Grandma Agatha patted Hannah's arm. "Thanks to you I have a reason to get up every morning. I thought I was useless to everyone, but I was wrong."

"You sure were!" Hannah chuckled. "When are you leaving for Detroit?"

"In three days."

Hannah hesitated, then asked, "Did you settle everything with Reid Meadows?"

"I don't know. I tried to call him today, but there was no answer." Grandma Agatha caught Hannah's hand and squeezed it. "I was wrong to hold a grudge all those years. It hurt me more than I ever realized." Grandma Agatha squeezed Hannah's hand again. "Don't let that happen to you. Eli told me what happened between you two. He's truly sorry. Don't hold a grudge against him, Hannah. It's not worth it. It'll eat away at you until you get rid of it. It doesn't disappear on its own just because you consciously forget it. It stays buried inside you, doing you more harm than you can imagine."

Hannah knew that what Grandma Agatha was saying was true. "I won't hold a grudge."

Smiling, Grandma Agatha hugged Hannah. "Good. Will I see you tomorrow?"

"I'll come over after school if you want."

"I'd like that. It's going to be hard to say good-bye to you." Grandma Agatha glanced toward the igloo. "I'll never forget our talk in the igloo."

"Me neither." Hannah suddenly wanted to keep Grandma Agatha as badly as she'd wanted to keep the igloo. "I wish you didn't have to go."

"But I do." Grandma Agatha smiled. "And I'll know how to have a wonderful time in Detroit—I'll share myself with my grandchildren just like I did here."

"I wish you were *my* grandma!"

Just then the door opened, and Alyson said sharply, "Telephone, Grandma Agatha. It's Reid Meadows."

Grandma Agatha flushed. "Thank you."

Hannah said good-bye and slowly walked toward home. She touched the igloo that was still ice-hard. She hesitated, then dropped down and crawled inside the tunnel. She poked her head into the igloo and stared in shock—Eli Shoulders sat there with his head in his hands.

Hannah's stomach flip-flopped, and she couldn't move.

13

Eli

Hannah wanted to creep out backwards without letting Eli know she was there, but she still couldn't move. Eli looked so sad! She slowly crawled all the way in. "Eli . . ." she said just above a whisper.

He jerked his head up and jabbed his glasses back into place. "Hannah!"

She sat at the edge of the carpet facing him. "Is something wrong?"

He studied her thoughtfully. "I didn't think you'd ever talk to me again."

"I know . . . but I forgave you."

He stabbed his fingers through his hair. "You wouldn't if you knew the whole truth."

Hannah stiffened. "The whole truth?"

Eli barely tipped his head. "The boys you saw yesterday dared me to ask you out to get you to answer the questions, and I took the dare. I know what you're thinking—I'm a jerk."

She waited for anger to rush over her, but none came. She smiled in relief. "It's over. I already forgave you."

"What a relief! Thanks."

"You don't have to be mad at yourself any longer either. I guess it's time you forgave yourself, don't you think?"

"I guess." Eli sighed heavily. "It's not easy to do when you've been such a jerk!"

"But you can do it with God's help."

"I know." Eli grinned. "Roxie's lucky to have you for a friend."

"Thanks."

He took a deep breath. "I still need to do my English assignment."

"Ask away." Had she really said that? She couldn't believe it!

His blue eyes widened behind his glasses. "Are you serious?"

"I guess I am." She laughed softly. "I can take it. Do you have the questions with you?"

"Yes, but no paper to write your answers on." He pulled a folded, crinkled paper from his jacket pocket. It looked like he'd wadded it up, then smoothed it out and folded it. "The questions are really dumb."

"I know."

"And you'll still answer them?"

"Sure. Why not? You need the grade, don't you?"

"Yes."

"Let's go to my house." Hannah crawled out of the igloo and waited for Eli. The sun was down, but it was still light enough to see.

He stood beside her and brushed snow off his knees. "Are you sure you want to do this?"

"I'll do it." She was glad she could talk to him without bursting into tears or getting angry. It wasn't his fault his teacher had given him this assignment.

"Roxie has said a lot of times she wishes she could be as nice as you. Now I see why she says that. You *are* nice, Hannah." Eli smiled.

Her pulse leaped, and she smiled back.

A few minutes later they sat at the kitchen table enjoying soda and chips. The younger girls were watching TV with Dad in the family room, while Mom was upstairs changing Burke. Dad had said the kitchen table was the best place for them to work.

Eli held a ballpoint pen over a sheet of paper. "You already answered the first question. Do you want to try again on the second one?"

Hannah took a deep breath. She hated the

question, but she hated the answer more. "We are all created equal, but sometimes we don't feel equal. I know I'm not always treated the same at school, so it makes me feel inferior to whites. I know I'm not, but I feel like it anyway."

Eli wrote for a long time. His handwriting was hard to read, and he dotted his *i*'s with a short slash. Finally he looked up. "Would you like to see more of your culture taught at school?"

"It doesn't matter to me. As Odawas we learn about our heritage from our elders. Some are proud of our heritage, and some aren't."

"Some say Odawas, and others say Ottawas. Why?"

"Some want to hang on to their language, so they say Odawa."

"Would you want others to know your heritage?"

"I guess it would help others to understand us more."

Eli laughed. "Is the answer yes or no?"

Hannah wrinkled her nose. "Yes."

"Would you rather marry a Native American or a white man?"

"I'll marry the man I love—the man God has for me."

"I can't write that down!"

"Why not? It's my answer. That's what you're supposed to get, right?"

Eli shrugged and wrote the answer. Then he asked, "What is the most wonderful thing about being Native American?"

"My family—all the people in my family, back to the grandparents. We help each other and are like one."

"What is the worst thing?"

"Having to fight to establish the right to have self-government. We are unrecognized because we have no land. We should have the right to keep our heritage alive—to try to get back some of what we lost. And we should not have lost what was ours in the first place."

"What do you want to be when you grow up?"

"I don't know. An artist. A teacher. Maybe a missionary." Hannah giggled. "Or a detective. What do you want to be?"

Eli looked off into space. "I don't want to be a carpenter or contractor like my dad. Maybe a professional athlete. That is, if I grow enough. I'm still too small." He looked at Hannah. "I hate being so small!"

"You don't seem small to me."

"Some boys are as big as men when they're sixteen, but I'm not."

"Your dad is tall, so you probably will be."

"That's what he says, but it's sure hard to wait." Eli sipped his soda. "I like talking to you, Hannah. If I did take a girl out, and if you were old enough to date boys, I'd ask you."

Hannah's heart soared. "You would?"

Smiling, Eli nodded. "You're easy to talk to." He slowly folded the papers and put them in the pocket of his jacket hanging on the back of his chair. "How well do you know Alyson?"

Hannah tensed. Was he going to say he'd like to go with her too? "Not very well."

"I tried to talk to her yesterday, but she's very hard to talk to. She seems really depressed. I'm afraid she might do something terrible."

"Like what?"

He flushed. "I don't know, but she really scared me. Have you noticed?"

"I guess not. But I really didn't pay attention."

"She reminds me of Susan Workman, Donna's sister. She likes the same music. And she feels life is worthless."

"That's terrible! Did you tell her grandma?"

Eli shook his head. "I didn't know how."

"Well, we've got to help her." Hannah's eyes flashed.

Eli chuckled. "You're already a missionary, aren't you?"

"I just know Jesus is the answer for them—and for us—for all of us." Hannah locked her hands in her lap and leaned toward Eli. "Are you sure about Alyson?"

Eli nodded.

"Why doesn't her family know?"

"Maybe nobody talks to her—I mean, really talks."

Tears welled up in Hannah's eyes. "I know I didn't." She'd been so busy being jealous, she hadn't gotten to know Alyson at all. "But I will, Eli! I mean it!"

"Good for you." He stood up and slipped on his jacket. "Thanks, Hannah."

"I hope you get an A on your assignment."

"Me too."

"Do you have to tell that you interviewed me, or can you just say it was a Native American?"

Eli frowned thoughtfully. "I don't know. I'll ask. Would you rather I didn't give your name?"

Hannah nodded. "Of course those boys who dared you know it's me, so they'll tell."

"You're right. I'm sorry, Hannah. I'll try never to take a dare again."

"Good." Hannah laughed as she walked Eli to the door. She opened it to let him out, then jumped in surprise. Grandma Agatha and Reid Meadows were standing there. "Hi! Come in."

"Hi," they said.

Eli said good-bye and ran across the street as Grandma Agatha and Reid Meadows stepped inside. Hannah closed the door, wondering why they had stopped in.

"Would you like a cup of tea or a glass of juice or something?" Hannah asked as she hung their coats in the closet.

"No thanks." Grandma Agatha shook her head at the same time Reid Meadows did. "We came to talk to you."

Hannah tensed as she led them into the living room where they could sit in comfort. "Is something wrong?" she asked around a dry throat.

Reid Meadows chuckled. "Just the opposite, thanks to you. Grandma Agatha is leaving for Detroit in three days, and I'm going there too. We'll get to see each other almost every day."

"We're considering getting married and living the rest of our lives together." Grandma Agatha smiled lovingly at Reid Meadows.

"But she needs more time before she can decide." Reid Meadows patted Grandma Agatha's hand. "I've already made up my mind."

Hannah stared at them in shock. She seldom thought of old people as wanting to get married. Ezra Menski had married Roxie's grandmother, but Hannah thought of that as an exception. "I don't know what to say."

Grandma Agatha laughed. "That's how I feel too, but I'll know soon. I'm praying for the answer."

Reid Meadows twisted the ring on his finger. "And it started with your sister finding my ring."

"And continued when I got rid of my grudge," Grandma Agatha said.

Hannah sat back and listened to Grandma Agatha and Reid Meadows. She considered saying something about Alyson, but couldn't just jump in and say it. She'd wait until Grandma Agatha was alone.

Was Alyson really thinking about doing something to end her life?

Hannah's stomach knotted even as she smiled at something Reid was saying.

14

Alyson

After school Hannah stopped beside the igloo and rubbed her hand over it. She'd been so afraid it would be melting after the warm sunny day. All the streets and most of the sidewalks were clear of snow, but the igloo hadn't melted. She smiled. "I'm glad you're still here."

She started to walk away when she heard muffled sobs. She frowned. Was she hearing things? She glanced around. Kids were running down the sidewalk toward their homes, their voices floating back. The students from The Ravines all met at and were dropped off at the end of the street by the yellow and black school bus, so it wouldn't have to drive through the subdivision.

Hannah leaned her head against the igloo. The sobs were coming from inside! Who would be crying in there? It wasn't Lena or the twins. They'd already gone inside the house for hot cocoa they knew Mom would have waiting for them.

Her heart racing, Hannah dropped to all fours at the opening of the tunnel. The snow was soft and very wet from the warm sun melting it. She crawled into the tunnel and peered into the igloo. Her eyes widened in surprise. Alyson Griggs was sitting on the carpet, crying into her hands.

"Alyson?"

She lifted her head. "Leave me alone!"

"No." Hannah sat on the edge of the carpet. "I want to help you."

"I don't want your help!" Alyson's blue eyes snapped. "You helped my little sisters, and you helped my grandma, and of course you helped little Donna Workman." Alyson flung her arms wide. "Now you want to help me. Don't bother!"

"Don't you think you're worth helping?"

"No, I'm not! Now leave me alone!"

"What upset you so much?"

Alyson pressed her lips tightly together. "Nosy, aren't you? All right, if you must know, I got caught cheating in math today. Do you know what my folks will do when they find out?"

"No. I know mine would punish me hard."

"Mine won't even answer the teacher's note! Mine don't care! Do you know that?"

Hannah couldn't imagine parents who didn't care. "What makes you think they don't care?"

"They never listen to me or take time for me. I've watched your parents and Chelsea's and Roxie's. I've seen you do things as a family. I've heard your mom play with your little sisters. My mom sets my little sisters in front of the TV and goes away."

"Tell your Grandma Agatha how you feel. She'll have a talk with your mom and dad."

"She'll be gone in a few days. What good would it do?"

"You can try."

"It doesn't do any good to try!" Alyson crawled past Hannah and out of the igloo, then ran to her house.

Hannah scrambled out into the open and jumped up. Should she follow Alyson? Hannah glanced at her watch. She was supposed to meet the Best Friends at Chelsea's house in twenty minutes. She'd take the time to tell Grandma Agatha what Eli had said about Alyson and what she'd said just now. Maybe Alyson would let her Grandma Agatha help her.

Hannah ran to the Griggs family's door and knocked. Brittany opened it. "Hi." Hannah smiled. "Is your Grandma Agatha home?"

"No."

Hannah's heart sank. "Your mom?"

"No."

Hannah frowned. "Who is?"

"Me and Alyson. She's in her room crying."

Hannah glanced back at Chelsea's house. She didn't have time for Alyson right now. Hannah bit her lip. She couldn't just forget about Alyson. With a sigh Hannah stepped inside. "I'll go talk to her."

"Okay."

"What are *you* going to do?"

Brittany shrugged hard.

"Where's Luann?"

"With Mom."

"When will your mom be home?"

Brittany shrugged again.

Hannah hugged Brittany. "Would you like to watch a video?"

"I guess so."

Hannah walked Brittany to the family room and helped her choose a video. Hannah turned it on for her and sat her down with a teddy bear. "I'll come see you after I finish talking to Alyson."

"Okay." Brittany hugged the teddy bear and watched the movie.

Slowly Hannah walked upstairs to find Alyson's bedroom. At the top of the steps Hannah stopped. Should she bother Alyson when she obviously didn't want to be bothered?

A picture of Susan Workman flashed across Hannah's mind. Susan had wanted help but didn't let anyone know. "I can't let Alyson do that," Hannah whispered.

Lifting her head in determination, Hannah walked down the hall until she heard sobs coming from a room.

Hannah knocked, then slowly turned the knob and opened the door. Clothes were strewn across the room. A plate with a half-eaten, dried-up doughnut sat on the dresser beside a pile of books. Depressingly dark posters hung on the walls.

Alyson jumped up from her bed and wiped at her teary eyes. "What are you doing here?"

"Helping you." Hannah draped her jacket over a chair and sat down.

"Even if I don't want help?"

"You want it all right. Nobody wants to feel miserable and sad."

Alyson flipped back her blonde hair. "How can you be nice to me after I've been so mean to you?"

"I just can."

Alyson sank to the edge of her bed. "Nobody cares about me. Nobody!"

"Jesus loves you."

Her eyes blazing, Alyson leaped to her feet. She shook her finger at Hannah. "Don't even start! I won't listen! I don't want to hear you talk about Jesus. Get out of my room!"

The rage in Alyson made Hannah tremble. "He wants to help you," Hannah said softly.

Alyson yanked Hannah up by her arm and shoved her toward the door. "Get out of here!"

"Let your Grandma Agatha help you."

"No!"

With tears in her eyes, Hannah ran downstairs, feeling defeated and embarrassed. As she reached to open the door, Grandma Agatha walked in, bringing cold air with her.

"I'm glad you're here," Grandma Agatha said with a cheerful smile.

Hannah brushed at her eyes to wipe away the tears. "I'm just leaving. I'm supposed to be at Chelsea's house right now."

"I wish you had time to talk." Grandma Agatha peered closely at Hannah. "You're upset. What happened?"

"Alyson . . . She's in her room . . . She didn't want help . . . Not my help anyway. Eli thinks she's like Susan Workman . . . Has her same . . . problem . . . Maybe you can talk to her."

"No. She doesn't like me much at all."

Grandma Agatha hung her coat in the closet. "I tried talking to her before."

"She doesn't think anyone cares!" Hannah knew she sounded frantic, but she couldn't help it. She *felt* frantic. "I think she'd talk to you if she knew you cared."

"I do care." Grandma Agatha smiled. "I didn't think I did, but I do. Yes, she does need to know I care." Grandma Agatha hugged Hannah close. "I'll try my best to help Alyson."

"Thank you!" Hannah said a quick good-bye and raced to Chelsea's bedroom to meet with the Best Friends. Roxie was leaning against the bed telling about gym class, Chelsea was sitting at her desk, and Kathy stood at the window. They all greeted Hannah at the same time. Before she could stop herself, Hannah burst into wild tears.

"Hannah!" The Best Friends clustered around her and tried to comfort her just as best friends should.

Finally Hannah was able to tell what had happened to upset her so much. "I tried to help her! I really tried!"

"Of course you did." Chelsea patted Hannah's back.

"I told her Jesus loves her and that He cares, but she shoved me out of her room!"

Kathy gripped Hannah's hand and looked into her face. "Listen to me, Hannah!"

"What?" Hannah's lip quivered.

"You didn't fail! You only started to help. And we'll all keep trying to help from now on."

Chelsea nodded. "We'll pray for her every day."

Roxie scowled. "And we'll rip those terrible posters off her wall!" Roxie giggled. "I guess we can't rip them off, but we can tell her how harmful they are to her. They depress her even more and make her think terrible things."

"Instead of life and hope and happiness," Hannah said, "she needs to know that Jesus wants to give her abundant life."

The Best Friends nodded. "We'll do our best to help her understand that."

Hannah looked at them and smiled, suddenly feeling better. She didn't have to help Alyson all by herself—the Best Friends would help her, and so would Grandma Agatha.

"Maybe Alyson would like to join *King's Kids*." Chelsea picked up her notebook with the list of kids who already belonged and the odd jobs they had done. "She needs to start hanging out with us."

Hannah sat with the Best Friends in Chelsea's room and made plans on ways to help Alyson

Griggs. Alyson was no longer alone, no matter what she thought right now. The Best Friends were there to help her, pray for her, and tell her about Jesus. That's what best friends do best.

Smiling, Hannah watched Chelsea open her notebook and write a list of all the things they would do for Alyson Griggs.

You are invited to become a
Best Friends Member!

In becoming a member you'll receive a club membership card with your name on the front and a list of the Best Friends and their favorite Bible verses on the back along with a space for your favorite Scripture. You'll also receive a colorful, 2-inch, specially-made I'M A BEST FRIEND button and a write-up about the author, Hilda Stahl, with her autograph. As a bonus you'll get an occasional newsletter about the upcoming BEST FRIENDS books.

All you need to do is mail your NAME, ADDRESS (printed neatly, please), AGE and $3.00 (U. S. currency only) for postage and handling to:

BEST FRIENDS
P.O. Box 96
Freeport, MI 49325

WELCOME TO THE CLUB!

(Authorized by the author, Hilda Stahl)